Elizabeth pressed a hand to her mouth, a tidal wave of nausea crashing over her. The body of a man in dark flannel trousers and a camel's hair cardigan lay facedown in the middle of the parlor floor; underneath him, the pale carpet was soaked with blood.

"It's him," Jessica gasped excitedly. "It's the dead man!"

Lucy Friday stood close to the corpse, looking down at it and reciting something into a hand-held tape recorder similar to Elizabeth's.

The side window was open a crack, and at that moment Lucy Friday's clear, dispassionate voice drifted out to them. The sight of the body was horrible enough, but her words were even more disturbing—they chilled Jessica and Elizabeth to the very bone. "The victim's throat has been ripped open," Lucy recorded, "as if by a wild beast. . . ."

SWEET VALLEY High

LOVE AND DEATH IN LONDON

Written by
Kate William

Created by
FRANCINE PASCAL

BANTAM BOOKS
NEW YORK · TORONTO · LONDON · SYDNEY · AUCKLAND

To Mia Pascal Johansson

RL 6, age 12 and up

LOVE AND DEATH IN LONDON
A Bantam Book / April 1994

Sweet Valley High® is a registered trademark of Francine Pascal
Conceived by Francine Pascal
Produced by Daniel Weiss Associates, Inc.
33 West 17th Street
New York, NY 10011
Cover art by Bruce Emmett

ISBN: 0-553-56227-4

Published simultaneously in the United States and Canada

Bantam Books are published by Bantam Books, a division of Bantam
Doubleday Dell Publishing Group, Inc. Its trademark, consisting of the
words "Bantam Books" and the portrayal of a rooster, is Registered in
U.S. Patent and Trademark Office and in other countries. Marca
Registrada. Bantam Books, 1540 Broadway, New York, New York 10036.

PRINTED IN THE UNITED STATES OF AMERICA

OPM   0 9 8 7 6 5 4 3 2 1

Chapter 1

"Look, Liz!" sixteen-year-old Jessica Wakefield cried with excitement. "I see England!"

Leaning across her twin sister, Elizabeth peered out the airplane window. Sure enough, the sparkling Atlantic Ocean had given way to a patchwork quilt of lush green farmland sprinkled with little villages. "England," Elizabeth breathed, clasping her hands together. "I can't believe we're really here!"

"We're not actually on the *ground* yet." Jessica bounced impatiently. "I feel as if I've spent my whole life on this plane. If I don't get off soon, I'll scream!"

Elizabeth was just as restless as her sister. It had been a long two days of traveling: they'd left Sweet Valley, California, on Saturday morning and switched planes in New York Saturday night. With the time change, the overnight flight to London was putting them into Heathrow Airport after lunch on Sunday.

"Just think," said Elizabeth. "Tomorrow we start our internships at the *London Journal*! It's going to be such a thrill to meet Mr. Reeves, to actually *work* with him."

Stars sparkled in Elizabeth's blue-green eyes. Jessica's eyes, meanwhile, crinkled up in a big yawn. *Elizabeth gets fired up about the strangest things*, Jessica thought. "Henry Reeves just looks like any old gray-haired geezer to me," she remarked carelessly.

Elizabeth looked shocked by Jessica's lack of awe and respect for the *Journal's* venerable editor-in-chief. "He's a *legend*, and the *London Journal* is the classiest, most intellectual newspaper in the world. This is an incredible honor. We're going to learn so much from him!"

"Well, I for one refuse to learn *too* much," Jessica declared. "It's summer vacation, after all— my brain cells need a rest."

"It won't be like school; it'll be fun," Elizabeth promised. "Remember what a blast we had interning for the *Sweet Valley News*? And that was just our local paper, ten minutes from home. This time we're going to be in London, *England*!"

Elizabeth sank back in her seat. The month-long internship aside, excitement enough for a would-be writer, a trip to England was a dream come true. "Think of all the wonderful poets and playwrights and novelists who were from England." Elizabeth listed the names rapturously.

2

"Wordsworth and Shelley and Keats. Charles Dickens and Jane Austen, Virginia Woolf, and the Brontë sisters. And Shakespeare!"

Jessica clapped her hands over her ears. "Don't even *speak* those names," she begged. "It makes me feel as if I'm back in Mr. Collins' English class. Remember, we're on *vacation*, Liz. V-A-C-A-T-I-O-N." She spelled out the word to give it a better chance of penetrating her sister's bookwormish brain. "Try not to be such a nerd, for once!"

Not surprisingly, the twins had very different reasons for looking forward to their stay in London. Although identical in appearance, with the same sun-kissed blond hair, turquoise eyes, and slim, athletic figures, their interests tended to propel them in opposite directions. Elizabeth made schoolwork a priority and spent hours every day writing for the Sweet Valley High newspaper, *The Oracle*, or in her journal. Jessica, on the other hand, inclined toward nonacademic activities like cheerleading, shopping, boy-watching, and sunbathing—she could only do homework if the stereo was blasting one of her favorite CDs, and if she took a break every five or ten minutes to yak on the phone with one of her friends. Elizabeth was a fixture of the Sweet Valley High party scene, but she also enjoyed spending quiet time with her best friend Enid Rollins, or Todd Wilkins, the boy she'd been dating steadily for as long as anyone could remember. Jessica had had a few steady boyfriends herself, but all in all preferred the life of a swinging single—why tie yourself down to just

3

one boy when the world was filled with so many cute ones?

"Our old boss from the *Sweet Valley News* was great to help us line up these internships, but let's get our agenda straight, OK?" said Jessica. "*I* plan to shop on Sloane Street, and hit the London music scene, and hobnob with royalty. *That's* what travel abroad is all about, if you ask me, not visiting musty old museums and making pathetic pilgrimages to the birthplaces of boring old authors who died *centuries* ago."

Elizabeth laughed. "Lucky for us, a city like London has something for everyone."

"It sure does. Remember the movie we watched at Lila's the other night?"

Elizabeth rolled her eyes. "How could I forget? *An American Werewolf in London*—nice choice for a friendly bon voyage party!"

Jessica laughed. "That girl has quite a sense of humor," she agreed. Lila had thrown a huge bash for the twins at her family's mansion, Fowler Crest, inviting everyone who was anyone at Sweet Valley High. A lot of people had worn costumes—the British royal family put in an appearance, as well as Sherlock Holmes and Watson, James Bond, and even Jack the Ripper. Lila had rented the horror movie *An American Werewolf in London*, and they'd all screamed themselves silly.

"Two teenaged American guys go to England on a backpacking trip and are attacked on the deserted moors by a werewolf." Jessica hugged herself, enjoying a pleasant shiver. "One of them's

4

ripped to shreds right then and there, but the other guy, David, lives and turns into a werewolf himself during the next full moon."

Elizabeth wrinkled her nose distastefully. "Really, Jess, do you have to remind me of all the gory details?"

"Yes, I do," said Jessica with a mischievous smile. "Because David ends up in *London* and goes on a total rampage, killing like half a dozen people before the entire London police force finally corners him in a dead-end alley and shoots him with a silver bullet. *Pow!*"

Elizabeth jumped. "Stop! You're scaring me all over again. Once was enough—I'd rather not even *think* about that movie."

"I liked it," Jessica declared with bloodthirsty relish. "Maybe there'll be a nice, ghoulish *murder* while we're working for the *London Journal*, something gruesome and creepy!"

Elizabeth shook her head. "Don't get your grisly hopes up," she advised. "It was just a movie, thank goodness!"

Just then, the head flight attendant's voice came over the intercom. "Please fasten your seat belts and bring your chairs to an upright position," she requested in a crisp British accent. "We've begun our descent into Heathrow and will be landing shortly."

Elizabeth and Jessica exchanged excited smiles. "Look out, London," announced Jessica. "Here we come!"

✿   ✿   ✿

"I love this, I absolutely love this," Elizabeth said twenty minutes later as they scurried through the bustling airport. Having passed through customs, they were headed for the baggage claim area. "Listen to that." Elizabeth stopped in her tracks and Jessica followed suit, cocking her ear. "English accents," Elizabeth explained when Jessica looked at her blankly. "Aren't they the coolest?"

"The coolest *and* the sexiest," Jessica agreed. "I just can't wait to meet some of these adorable English boys!"

Thirty seconds later, it was Jessica's turn to slam on the brakes. "Liz! Is that who I think it is?"

She pointed to a tall, elegantly dressed young man with a thatch of unruly chestnut hair, ruddy cheeks, and a wide grin. "I don't know. Who *do* you think it is?" replied Elizabeth.

"A prince," Jessica gushed. "Or the cousin of a prince, or at least the *friend* of a prince . . ."

Grabbing her sister's arm, Elizabeth dragged her forward. "Not every good-looking rich guy in England will turn out to be a member of the royal family, you know."

"No, but some of them are bound to." Jessica's gaze was already roving in search of more potential celebrities. "They're out there somewhere! Isn't it just great to be in a country where there are kings and queens and *aristocrats*?"

They reached the baggage carousel to find a mob of travelers waiting for luggage to begin appearing. Wandering over to a row of newspaper

6

vending machines, Jessica and Elizabeth halted in front of the first one. "Speaking of the royal family," Elizabeth said, "take a look at those headlines!"

Every newspaper on display, including the *London Journal*, trumpeted the same startling news. "'Princess Eliana Missing,'" Jessica read out loud. "Wow, that's terrible!"

"Here." Elizabeth fumbled in her pocket for some change. "Let's buy a paper." She started to stick a quarter in the slot, then caught herself with a laugh. "I almost forgot—we need to trade in our American money for British currency! Be right back."

While Elizabeth dashed off to the currency exchange, Jessica bent over to look at the grainy black-and-white picture accompanying the *Journal*'s story about the missing princess. An unsmiling, fair-haired girl stared out at Jessica from the front page. "Missing," Jessica breathed. "I wonder where she is? Did she run away? Was she kidnapped?"

Elizabeth had returned with a handful of pound notes and coins. "We'll find out," she said, inserting a coin and removing a copy of the *Journal*.

Their heads close together, the twins read eagerly about the disappearance of the British queen's youngest daughter. "She looks spoiled and bored," Elizabeth commented, examining the photo.

"According to this, she's 'a darling of the British press and public,'" Jessica quoted. "And did you know she's sixteen, exactly our age?"

"They don't have any clues to her whereabouts—there's been no ransom note, nothing." Elizabeth shivered. "Pretty scary, huh?"

Behind them, they heard a beeping sound. The luggage from their flight began to roll onto the conveyor belt. Tucking the newspaper under her arm, Jessica hurried over just in time to snatch her suitcase as it rumbled by.

When Elizabeth's appeared a moment later, they were ready to head outside and hail a cab. "Look at the big, black taxis!" Jessica squealed. "Aren't they wild?"

They joined the queue waiting for a cab and soon were being helped into one of the spacious, lumbering Austins by a burly driver. "Americans, I see," he grunted cheerfully through his thick black beard. He tossed Elizabeth's bag into the trunk as if it weighed no more than a feather. "Is this your first visit to London?"

Elizabeth and Jessica nodded. Shutting them into the backseat, the driver returned to the wheel and revved the engine. "I suppose you've heard about the missing princess," he remarked as they merged with the traffic heading for the city. "Biggest story in years."

Jessica gasped suddenly, clutching Elizabeth's arm. "Stop!" she shrieked at the cabbie. "You're driving on the wrong side of the road!"

To her surprise, a bearlike chuckle rumbled from his chest. "We drive on the left side in England," he informed her, "and that's the *right* side, in our view."

Jessica collapsed weakly against the seat. "I'll

never get used to it," she told her sister.

"Me, neither," Elizabeth admitted. "I keep thinking we're going to have a head-on collision!"

A short, swift ride took them from the outskirts of London into the heart of the city. Jessica and Elizabeth looked from one side of the taxi to the other, devouring the exciting new sights and sounds. "Look, it's the Parliament buildings and Big Ben!" Elizabeth pointed to the famous clock.

"You said Winchester Street, didn't you, miss?" the cabdriver called back.

"That's right." Elizabeth glanced again at the brochure from HIS, Housing for International Students, the room-and-board youth hostel where they'd live during their internships. "One thousand and twenty Winchester Street."

"A safe enough neighborhood," the cabbie said approvingly. "But mind you don't wander around the city overmuch by yourselves. It's easy for strangers to lose their way, and scenic as it is, London can be a dangerous place." He made a worried tsking sound. "I fear the worst for the young princess, I'll tell you that."

Elizabeth clasped her hands together tightly, sobered by the cabbie's warning. Jessica tossed her hair, unconcerned. "We'll be fine," she said carelessly. "It's not like we've never been away from home before."

The taxi began winding its way through a spiderweb of tree-lined residential streets. "Nevertheless," the cabbie insisted, "you don't want to learn your lessons the hard way. Don't forget to

9

look both ways before crossing the street—the traffic comes from the right, not the left the way you're used to. I've seen more than one of my American passengers leave the taxi and nearly lose their lives with their first step in London."

With those ominous if well-intended words, the driver coasted to a stop in front of an unadorned yet elegant brick Georgian house. "Here you are," he announced.

As she paid the cabdriver, Elizabeth realized her heart was pounding with nervous anticipation. Jessica gave her sister's hand a quick squeeze and then flung open the door of the taxi, not waiting for the driver to assist her.

She stepped onto the curb with Elizabeth close at her heels. Staring eagerly ahead at the group of young people gathered on the front steps of HIS, Jessica didn't notice the hunchbacked old bag lady hobbling along the sidewalk toward her until they were face-to-face. The woman was dressed in grimy rags, and her wildly tangled gray hair looked as if it might provide a home for bats. Jessica yelped in surprise.

"Beware the full moon," the old woman hissed, her wart-covered nose just inches from Jessica's. "Beware the full moon."

The bag lady hobbled on without a backward glance. Jessica shook her head, laughing at herself for being so startled, but Elizabeth couldn't quite muster a smile. As she watched the old crone disappear around the corner, an unaccountable shiver chased up her spine.

Chapter 2

"Are you coming, Liz?" Jessica asked.

Elizabeth took a deep breath, shaking off the creepy sensation. Bending, she picked up the suitcase the cabbie had deposited on the curb.

A dozen boys and girls were hanging out in front of the youth hostel, chatting and laughing. Some were speaking English, but Elizabeth also heard French and German—even what she thought might be Russian.

"This is so cool!" Jessica whispered in Elizabeth's ear. "Kind of like an international version of Sweet Valley High. Check out that gorgeous guy on the left—he's *got* to be Italian!"

As the twins approached, the other teenagers stopped talking and looked at them curiously. "Hi," said Jessica.

They were greeted by smiles and a chorus of hellos in various languages.

11

An auburn-haired girl with a splash of freckles across her upturned nose hopped to her feet and stepped up to the twins. "You must be the Americans," she guessed, her emerald-green eyes twinkling with friendliness. Grabbing Jessica's suitcase with one hand, she opened the front door with the other. "You're just in time for tea," she announced, striding across the foyer to the staircase. "I promise we won't bore you with tales of the missing princess. Stash your stuff in your room and then come on!"

There didn't seem to be anything to do but to chase after the red-haired girl. "I'm Elizabeth Wakefield and this is my sister, Jessica," Elizabeth said.

"Of course you are. Oh, I'm sorry!" The girl burst out laughing, her eyes crinkling. "Emily Cartwright. Nice to meet you."

"Your accent," said Jessica. "It's not English, it's . . ."

"Australian. I'm from Sydney. Lovely town, if I may say so myself." They paused on the second-floor landing to catch their breath. "I'm taking you all the way up to three," Emily said. "That's where the girls are—the boys are on two. Mrs. Bates is putting you in with Lina and Portia. It's a big airy room—you'll like it fine."

"What brings you to London?" Elizabeth asked Emily as they continued up the stairs.

"An internship at the BBC—the British Broadcasting Company," Emily replied. "I'd like to go into television production."

12

Trooping down the blue-carpeted third-floor hallway, Emily stopped at the last door on the left, nudging it open with her foot.

Jessica and Elizabeth peeked inside eagerly. The room had two sets of bunk beds, one made up with sheets and blankets and the other bare with the linens folded and stacked on top. There were two dressers, and one corner of the room had been turned into a conversation nook with easy chairs, a coffee table, and a reading lamp. A door stood open, revealing a walk-in closet already half full of clothes, shoes, and other feminine odds and ends. White lace curtains fluttered at the open windows, and the scent of a delicate floral perfume filled the air.

"Top or bottom bunk?" Elizabeth asked, dropping her suitcase on the floor with a thump.

"Top," said Jessica.

Emily made herself comfortable in one of the easy chairs. "Pretty room, isn't it?" she chattered. "I've got both good and bad news about your roommates, however. The good news is Lina Smith—she's a real sweetie pie. The bad news is Portia Albert. *She's* a royal pain in the you-know-what."

Jessica and Elizabeth laughed.

"Lina's from a poor family in Liverpool," Emily went on, without pausing for breath. "She's working for the summer at a homeless shelter and soup kitchen. They only pay her pennies and she doesn't get much help from home, so I really don't know how she manages. You'll like her," Emily promised. "She comes across as a bit quiet and shy, but she's got a bold streak."

"What about Portia?" prompted Jessica.

Emily rolled her eyes. "*Portia* is the daughter of Sir Montford Albert. Have you heard of him?"

"Have we *heard* of him?" Elizabeth squealed. "He's the most famous Shakespearean actor in the *world*!"

"So, you can imagine how stuck-up Portia is," said Emily. "She came to London from Edinburgh, where her dad runs a theater company, to be an actress herself. I've never met a snobbier, ruder, more self-absorbed girl in my life."

"Then you've never met Lila Fowler," Jessica kidded, referring to her best friend and chief rival at Sweet Valley High.

"Is she really that bad?" wondered Elizabeth as she unzipped her suitcase and started placing her clothes in the bottom dresser drawers.

"Ask anyone in the dorm." Slinging one slender leg over the arm of the chair, Emily swung her foot idly. "Nobody can stand her. She thinks she's the bee's knees because she landed a part in a new play opening later this week in the West End—thanks to Sir Montford's influence, I don't doubt."

"So, what's it like living here?" asked Jessica. Her unpacking technique differed somewhat from Elizabeth's; she simply held her suitcase upside down and shook its contents unceremoniously on the bed. "How's the food? Are there a lot of rules?"

"The food is plain but there's plenty of it. A big English breakfast at eight, tea from four in the afternoon till six, and a light supper later. You're on your own for lunch. As for *rules* . . . Didn't I mention Mrs. Bates, the housemother, is the epitome of ironclad propriety? If you want to stay on her good side—not that she has one, mind you—you'd better plan to follow HIS rules to the *letter*."

As she and Elizabeth exchanged a glance, Jessica smiled slyly. *Follow the rules, eh? Talk about an invitation to do just the opposite!*

"No boys on the third floor," Emily elaborated, "and the girls aren't to linger on the second-floor landing *or* to set foot—not a single toe!—into the second-floor hallway. Then there's the *curfew*."

Jessica wrinkled her nose. "Curfew?"

"Curfew," Emily repeated. "Eleven o'clock, and Mrs. Bates locks and bolts the front door promptly. If you're not inside, you'll spend the night on the street."

"I can't believe we have a curfew," Jessica complained to Elizabeth. "We might as well still be at home!"

"That's the whole point," Elizabeth reminded her. "Why do you think Mom and Dad *picked* this place for us?"

"You'll meet Mrs. Bates at tea, and I'm sure she'll go over everything." Emily cocked her head to one side. "You're the first Americans this summer—I wonder how she'll treat you? It's highly possible you won't be up to snuff in her book. She fawns over Portia because she's got 'bloodlines,' but she's a bit chilly to the rest of us." Emily laughed heartily. "Especially me, being from Australia. 'Why, my dear, do you *know* who your ancestors are? The whole *country* was settled by *convicts*!'"

15

Emily's laughter was contagious, and Elizabeth and Jessica joined in. "She sounds like a real ogre," Elizabeth commented, hanging two cotton dresses in the closet. "I'm almost afraid to go down to tea!"

"She takes good care of us, in her own way," Emily assured her. "And you *mustn't* skip tea—it's the perfect time to meet the rest of the gang, and it's a grand bunch." Checking her watch, she hopped to her feet. "In fact, tea is served in five minutes. Let's go down to the dining room, shall we?"

Sticking their empty suitcases under the bottom bunk, the twins sped off in Emily's energetic wake. "Now that you know about a few of the girls, I'll tell you about some of the boys. David Bartholomew is from Liverpool, like Lina. His mum's a charwoman and his father is on the dole— disability, I think. He's attending the London University summer session on a scholarship, studying literature. Quite the serious, bookish young man—a very nice fellow."

They reached the second-floor landing, and Elizabeth fought off the urge to dash into the hallway in violation of Mrs. Bates's stern rules. "Gabriello Moretti's at the university, too, taking a summer course in music," Emily continued. "Classical, but he also plays rock. He's Italian and gorgeous, an absolute work of art." She winked playfully. "Michelangelo's David springs to mind."

Jessica's eyes sparkled with interest. "Sounds like the boy of my dreams."

"Sorry." Emily patted Jessica's arm. "He already found a girlfriend—Sophie from the summer ses-

16

sion—it took him about five minutes. But *Rene* . . . I don't think *he's* attached."

"Rene?" said Jessica.

"From France. He's interning at the embassy." Emily sighed dreamily. "He's handsome and charming and, well, *French*, if you know what I mean."

Rene from France . . . At the sound of the name, Elizabeth's heart skipped a beat. Apparently, Jessica had the same thought. "Rene," Jessica whispered in Elizabeth's ear as they reached the bottom of the staircase. "Do you think it could be . . . ?"

Elizabeth put a hand to her face. It grew hot as she felt herself transported back to the spring break she and Jessica had spent as exchange students in southern France. They'd stayed in Cannes at the home of Madame Avery Glize and her son, Rene, while Rene's sister, Fernie, visited the Wakefields in Sweet Valley.

At first, the twins found Rene unfriendly to the point of rudeness. It turned out that he resented Americans because his American father had divorced his mother and, after remarrying and starting a new family in the States, he'd wanted nothing to do with the family he'd left behind. Elizabeth had finally managed to break through Rene's defenses, however. *I'll never forget what a hero he was,* Elizabeth thought, pressing the palm of her hand to her pink cheek. *That day he overcame his fear of water to save Jessica's life after the sailing accident. And then we kissed. . . .*

She'd returned to Sweet Valley before anything

17

had a chance to develop with Rene, and that was just as well, as she had a boyfriend at home. But Elizabeth had always wondered. *What if . . . ?*

"It can't be him," she whispered back. "There must be a million Renes in France."

But as they walked into the oak-paneled dining room a moment later, there he was, standing by the bay window with a steaming cup of tea in his hand. His dark eyes moved to Jessica and Elizabeth as they entered and instantly lit up with pleased recognition. Putting his cup down, he crossed the room with long, quick strides. "Elizabeth and Jessica Wakefield!"

"Rene, fancy meeting you here!" Jessica cried.

As Emily watched in astonishment, Rene took both Jessica's hands in his and kissed her with enthusiasm twice, first on the left cheek and then on the right. "What a wonderful surprise," he exclaimed, turning to Elizabeth.

Releasing Jessica's hands, he seized Elizabeth's, squeezing them warmly. "Elizabeth, you haven't changed a bit," Rene murmured as he bent to kiss her. Did she imagine it, or did his lips seem to linger on her cheek? "Except, *si c'est possible*, you've grown even more beautiful."

Rene's dark eyes smiled down at her, and Elizabeth blushed. *Si c'est possible*, you're *even taller and more handsome*, she could have responded. "This is such an incredible coincidence," she gasped instead.

"We have to sit and talk," he declared. Taking

18

Elizabeth's arm, Rene led the three girls to a table by the window. As he dashed off to pour tea and fill plates with sandwiches and cookies, Emily leaned forward to whisper to the twins.

"I can't believe you already know the cutest boy in the dorm!"

Jessica lifted her hands and smiled smugly. "What can we say?"

Rene returned with the tea. As he handed Elizabeth her cup, his fingers brushed lightly against hers, making her skin tingle. "I know you've probably just arrived, but before Emily whirls you away to meet everybody else, you must tell me how you've been and what brings you to London," he said. "It's been too long since we corresponded."

"Jessica and I have summer internships at the *London Journal*," Elizabeth told him.

"Ah. You still want to be a writer."

Elizabeth smiled. "And you?"

"My interests have been changing and evolving lately," Rene replied. "You see, I've reconciled with my father."

Elizabeth touched his arm, her eyes glowing. "I'm so glad to hear that!"

"Fernie and I visited him and his second family in Massachusetts, and recently he invited me along on a business trip to Japan," said Rene, choosing a small egg-salad sandwich. "All this travel has given me the idea that I might like to study international relations when I go to university next year."

"Emily says you have an internship at the

19

French embassy," said Elizabeth. "Are you enjoying it?"

"Immensely," Rene told her. "But it's very busy. Almost every night, I have to attend a reception or function of some sort."

"We never see him," Emily confirmed as she reached for the pitcher and sloshed some milk into her tea.

"But now that *you're* here . . ." Rene smiled at Jessica and then turned his gaze on Elizabeth, staring deep into her eyes. "I'll just have to make some free time."

Elizabeth felt Jessica kick Emily under the table and blushed furiously. She had a boyfriend at home—she was in love with Todd Wilkins, and always would be. But she couldn't deny it; the sparks were still there between her and Rene Glize.

She'd arrived in London just that afternoon, and it looked as if the first adventure of the summer was starting already!

"I am *so* tired, I think I could sleep for a *year*," Jessica moaned as she and Elizabeth walked slowly up the stairs to the third floor.

"Your internal clock is all mixed up—jet lag," Elizabeth said, yawning widely.

After supper, the sisters had hung out for an hour in the library gabbing with some of their new housemates. There were two people they still had yet to meet, however: Lina and Portia. According to Emily, Portia usually missed tea and dinner because of play rehearsals. As for Lina, the twins had only gotten a glimpse of her, when she ducked late into tea, grabbed a scone, and hurried off again.

They found the door to their room ajar. As they entered, Lina Smith turned toward them, in the act of slipping her arms out of a worn gray wool cardigan.

"Why, hullo!" she said in a cheery Liverpudlian accent reminiscent of the Beatles. "You must be Jessica and Elizabeth. I hope I didn't seem overly rude at tea, not stopping by to introduce myself properly, but it was my night to captain the soup kitchen supper crew and I had to dash right back out."

Lina was a slender girl of medium height with cropped brown hair and big blue eyes sparkling intelligently behind wire-rimmed glasses. Elizabeth liked her immediately. "It's nice to meet you," Elizabeth said. "The soup kitchen must be hard work."

Lina flopped down into one of the easy chairs and kicked off her loafers. "It's exhausting, but also rewarding. I don't know what could be more satisfying than providing needy people with a square meal and a clean, safe bed." She heaved a sigh. "Unless, of course, we found a way to eliminate homelessness altogether."

"It's a problem in the U.S., too," said Elizabeth, hunting in her drawer for a nightgown.

"Well, what is *your* government doing about it?" Lina sat forward, her elbows on her knees and her eyes flashing. "Do you think the American political system is better constituted to cure social ills than the British system? Because I think we English tend to . . ."

As she and Lina talked politics, Elizabeth could see Jessica fighting to suppress a yawn—and losing the battle. It didn't take Jessica long to categorize people, and Elizabeth could tell her sister had already decided she had nothing in common with unglamorous Lina in her plain navy-blue dress and gray knee socks; spunky, flashy Emily the undisputed gossip queen of HIS was more Jessica's style. *Although with a bit of a fashion make-over, Lina would be very pretty,* Elizabeth found herself musing. *She reminds me of someone . . . but who?*

At that moment, the door to the bedroom was flung wide open from the other side. As it banged against the wall, Lina shot an ironic glance at Jessica and Elizabeth. "Here comes her royal highness," she whispered.

A tall, curvy girl with a cascade of wavy raven-black hair took one step into the room and then paused dramatically, surveying the scene through lowered lashes. Disdainful gray eyes raked Jessica and Elizabeth up and down. "Twins. How quaint," the girl drawled, as if to herself.

She breezed across the room without another glance at the girls. "Portia, this is Elizabeth and Jessica Wakefield, our new roommates from California," said Lina.

"Hmm," Portia murmured, stripping off her unstructured raw silk jacket and flinging it into the closet. "Delighted, I'm sure."

She sounded anything but. Elizabeth looked at Lina. Lina shrugged as if to say, *Your move, if you really want to make one.*

"We hear you're an actress," Elizabeth ventured, addressing Portia's back. "Emily says you have a role in a new play."

Flouncing from the closet to her dressing table, Portia sat down in front of the mirror, her back still pointedly turned to Elizabeth, Jessica, and Lina. "Hmm, yes."

Elizabeth made another attempt. "Actually, my sister's very interested in theater, aren't you, Jess? She's a member of the drama club at school. And I just love reading plays in English class, especially Shakespeare," Elizabeth rambled on.

Slowly, Portia pivoted in her chair and fixed Elizabeth with a withering look. "We *must* continue this fascinating chat sometime," she said in the haughtiest British accent Elizabeth had ever heard. "A cultural discussion with Americans, whose idea of theater is the thirty-minute situation comedy, promises to be immensely . . . *refreshing.*"

With that, Portia faced the mirror again and began removing her makeup. After brushing her hair for thirty strokes, she undressed and slipped into an elegant, lace-trimmed satin nightgown. "I do hope you're ready for lights-out," she announced, her hand hovering over the light switch.

Quickly, Jessica, Elizabeth, and Lina scrambled into their sleep attire. Lina and Jessica hopped into the top bunks and grinned across at each other, smothering giggles.

23

Elizabeth watched, fascinated, as Portia pulled back her covers, climbed into bed, donned eyeshades and earplugs, and then lay gracefully back on her pillow. *Emily wasn't exaggerating,* she marveled silently. *Portia's everything she promised, and more!*

For fifteen minutes, the room had been dead quiet. *They're all asleep,* Elizabeth thought, rolling over in her bed to face the window.

The waxing moon shone brightly, bathing Elizabeth's face in eerie light. The night breeze, as soft as a sigh, lifted the curtains gently and then let them drop again. Elizabeth was bone tired, but she couldn't sleep. Her head whirled with thoughts of home and her parents and Todd . . . and Rene and what the next day would bring.

"Jessica?" Elizabeth whispered after a moment, hoping her twin was still awake.

"Hmm?" Jessica mumbled sleepily from the top bunk.

"What do you think that old woman on the sidewalk meant when she said 'Beware the full moon'?"

The bunk creaked as Jessica rolled over. "She meant beware of werewolves, of course. Remember the line from *An American Werewolf in London*? The villagers tried to warn the Americans about werewolves, but they didn't listen. And look what happened to them!"

Jessica's tone was lighthearted and teasing, but Elizabeth felt spooked. "You don't *believe* in werewolves, do you?" she asked, pulling her covers up to her chin and eyeing the moon with apprehension.

A muffled snort floated down from the top bunk. "*I* don't," Jessica said, "but obviously that nutty lady did!" She howled softly, and they both broke up laughing.

Chapter 3

Monday morning dawned wet and cool and foggy. "Pretty different from summer in Sweet Valley," Jessica said to Elizabeth as they dug into their hearty breakfast of eggs, sausage, and baked tomatoes. "Does it rain here all the time, you guys?"

"Pretty often," Lina acknowledged, digging into a bowl of muesli. "I can't imagine living someplace where it's always warm and sunny. No wonder you two are so bronzed."

Jessica felt a momentary pang, thinking about how she would while away the first day of summer vacation if she were back in Sweet Valley. *I'd sleep until noon and then head to the beach with Lila and Amy, where we'd spend hours just lounging on the white sand, reading fashion magazines and scoping guys.* "By the end of this internship, I'll have lost my tan completely and be pale as a ghost," Jessica predicted mournfully.

"A month in London is worth it, though, don't you think?" said Emily.

"Yes, we'll try to make it up to you," promised Lina.

Jessica's expression brightened. "Maybe I'll cultivate the pale, aristocratic look of a British royal," she mused. Imitating the newspaper photo of the missing princess, she pursed her lips in a sulky, blue-blooded pout.

Lina smiled. "That's it exactly."

After finishing breakfast, the four girls bused their dishes and headed into the front hall, where they converged with David and Gabriello. Only Portia still lingered in bed, having grumbled about how much noise the twins and Lina made getting ready for work earlier.

"I'm off to the BBC," Emily declared, sauntering out to the sidewalk. "Have fun at the *Journal*, Liz and Jess. Can't wait to hear all about it!"

Elizabeth and Jessica waved after Emily, then turned to bid good-bye to Lina; the soup kitchen was in the opposite direction. "See you tonight!" Lina called back to them.

David and Gabriello shouldered backpacks weighted down with books; Gabriello also carried a violin case. "We're walking to the corner to catch the bus to the university," said Gabriello, shaking back his shaggy black hair. "How about you?"

"We take the tube," Elizabeth told him. "Have a good day, guys."

"The tube—that's such a funny name," Jessica chattered as she and Elizabeth walked toward the street and prepared to cross. "Why don't they just call it a subway? I mean, isn't it the same thing?"

Looking over her shoulder, Jessica tossed one last wave to Gabriello and David and then stepped off the curb. A piercing horn sounded and Elizabeth grabbed Jessica's arm, yanking her back onto the sidewalk with a warning cry. "Jessica, watch out!"

A blood-red double-decker bus roared past them, right over the spot where Jessica had been standing only an instant before. Jessica gasped. "You looked the wrong way, just like the cabdriver said you would!" Elizabeth exclaimed, giving her sister's arm a shake. "You'd better be more careful. Do you want to get *killed* on your first day in London?"

Jessica took a deep breath, trying to slow her racing heartbeat. Shaken by this close call, she looked both ways with exaggerated care. "How come it's always me who makes all the dumb mistakes?" she muttered as she and Elizabeth scurried across the street and continued on their way to the *Journal*.

"This part of the city is very ancient and historical," Elizabeth told Jessica as they walked from the tube station to the offices of the *London Journal*. "It was laid out in the seventeenth century by the famous architect Sir Christopher Wren, after a big fire burned most of London down to the ground. The streets are like spokes in a wheel, all radiating outward from St. Paul's Cathedral."

29

They stopped in front of a tall building with the newspaper's name blazoned over the door. "This is it." Elizabeth patted the shoulder bag, which held a notebook and her new miniature tape recorder. "Ready to report some news, Jess?"

They pushed through the revolving door to find the newspaper office in chaos. Past the reception desk, the twins could see *Journal* staffers running to and fro like hamsters in a cage. "We're looking for the editor-in-chief, Henry Reeves," Elizabeth told the receptionist. "He's expecting us. We're—"

The receptionist waved them in without bothering to take their names. "Go ahead. If you can find him, more power to you."

"I wonder what's going on?" Jessica whispered as they made their way through a sea of desks. Telephones were ringing everywhere, and the hum of voices and clattering computer keyboards was deafening.

"A big story must be breaking," Elizabeth surmised, her heart leaping with excitement. "Let's find out!"

"Excuse me." Elizabeth waved to catch the attention of a young woman sprinting by. "We're looking for—"

The woman didn't even break stride to glance at the twins. "Excuse me, sir," Elizabeth tried again, this time reaching out to touch an older man's sleeve. "Can you tell me where—"

The man brushed past her. "Ask the receptionist."

Jessica had a different tactic. Planting herself squarely in front of the next person to approach, she put her hands on her hips and demanded loudly, "What's all the fuss about?"

The middle-aged woman, her gray hair flying in every direction, stopped just long enough to say, "You mean you haven't heard? It appears that Cameron Neville, a prominent London doctor, was murdered last night. His body was discovered only *minutes* ago!"

Clutching an armful of manila folders, the woman bustled off. Jessica and Elizabeth gaped at each other. "A *murder*," Jessica squeaked.

"Looks like your wish is coming true," said Elizabeth, referring to her sister's flip remark on the plane.

"Maybe Henry Reeves will put us on the story!" Jessica said hopefully.

Elizabeth couldn't deny that this prospect was very appealing. *We'd work with Scotland Yard to solve the case,* she fantasized. *Our story would be on the front page and we'd have our very own by-lines: 'Reported exclusively for the* Journal *by Elizabeth and Jessica Wakefield'!*

"Henry Reeves can't put us on *any* story if we don't find him and introduce ourselves, though," she pointed out.

"Which may never happen, as everybody in this crazy office is ignoring us." Jessica craned her neck. "I'm going to the ladies' room and reapply some lipstick—be right back."

As Jessica disappeared in the direction of the rest rooms, Elizabeth continued the search for Henry Reeves. "He'd have a private office, of course," she murmured to herself, walking down one of the short hallways that sprouted out from the central office space. She peeked into a couple of empty conference rooms. "Maybe around this corner . . ."

Around the bend, the hallway ended in a large, open work area. Here, away from the frantic activity of the main office, a boy sat alone at a desk, writing in a notebook. "Excuse me," Elizabeth began, her voice sounding loud in the silence.

The boy jumped, startled. Slamming his notebook shut, he looked up at Elizabeth. Their eyes locked.

His were a clear, alpine-lake blue. His skin was fair and his hair, a long lock of which fell over his forehead, was almost black. He reminded Elizabeth of pictures she'd seen of the Romantic poet Lord Byron, and she caught her breath.

"I—I'm sorry if I startled you, but I was wondering whether you could tell me—"

Before she could finish her question, the boy sprang to his feet, still staring at her, his face pale and frightened as if he'd seen a ghost. Elizabeth would have repeated her apology, but she didn't get a chance. "I must . . . take care of something," the boy muttered vaguely. Then he bolted past her and disappeared.

Still puzzling over the strange encounter, Elizabeth retraced her steps. She bumped into her sister halfway. "I found Henry Reeves," Jessica declared triumphantly. "Come on!"

Together, they hurried to the editor-in-chief's

office. The door was wide open, and Henry Reeves was inside, talking to two of his reporters.

Elizabeth recognized him immediately from the photograph in a recent magazine article about the world's most influential newspaper publishers and editors. Under the stewardship of Henry Reeves, the *London Journal* had won a slew of journalistic honors and consolidated its position as the most widely read paper in England.

The three men continued their discussion, in argumentative tones, as Jessica and Elizabeth approached. Elizabeth cleared her throat. "Excuse me," she said hesitantly. "Mr. Reeves?"

The tall, silver-haired editor-in-chief turned toward her impatiently. "What do you want?" he snapped.

Elizabeth blinked. "Uh, I'm Elizabeth Wakefield and this is my sister, Jessica," she stuttered, shifting her feet. When Mr. Reeves stared at her without comprehension, she added, "We're the new summer interns from Sweet Valley High. We—we *were* supposed to start today, weren't we?"

"Yes, of course, today's fine. Just stay out of the way," Mr. Reeves said briskly. "Get over to Frank in society—the desk by the east window—tell him he can do whatever he wants with you."

With a distracted, shooing gesture, Mr. Reeves hustled Jessica and Elizabeth out of his office and slammed the door. The twins gaped at each other. "He acted like he'd never even heard our names before!" Jessica said, her eyes flashing indignantly. "What a jerk!"

Elizabeth's shoulders slumped with disappointment. So much for her dreams of working with Scotland Yard and being personally mentored by Henry Reeves, the perfect English gentleman-editor. "He's not what I expected," she conceded glumly. "I thought he'd have special assignments for us—I thought he'd take us under his wing."

"Instead, he's shoving us aside like unwanted furniture. This internship is really getting off to a great start," Jessica complained as they trooped back across the office. "I can't believe we flew all the way across the ocean to be assigned to the *social* page! Society," she muttered disdainfully as they stepped up to a cubicle with a nameplate reading: TONY FRANK, SOCIETY EDITOR. "What's that, tea parties?"

A sandy-haired man in a wrinkled blue Oxford shirt glanced up at the twins. His mouth twisted in a sardonic smile. "They're not just *any* tea parties, mind you, but the tea parties of the very rich and well-bred," he said dryly. "The *aristocracy*." He drew the word out, giving it a nasal, hoity-toity inflection. Elizabeth and Jessica giggled. "By the way, I don't think I've had the pleasure."

"Oh!" Elizabeth laughed. "We're Elizabeth and Jessica Wakefield, new interns from—"

Tony Frank held up a hand. "Let me guess." He grinned. "Sunny California."

"Bingo," said Jessica.

"So, how can I help you?" he asked, sitting on the edge of his desk.

"Mr. Reeves sent us over," Elizabeth explained.

"He didn't seem to remember that we were coming. He said to tell you you could do whatever you wanted with us."

"Ah." Tony Frank tapped a pencil on the desk. "And writing for the society column isn't exactly what you had in mind."

"Not really," Jessica confessed.

"Well, I don't like it any better than you do." Tony Frank's eyes glittered with sudden fire. "What I wouldn't give to get my hands on a story like the Dr. Neville murder. . . ." He refocused on the twins, a thoughtful smile on his lips. "Tell you what. Since Reeves doesn't seem to care what you do, let's see if we can't drum up something a little more interesting than tea parties."

Once again, Jessica and Elizabeth plunged into the whirl of the *Journal*. Following Tony, they made their way to a cubicle on the opposite side of the office. A big white storyboard was labeled: CRIME.

"Crime—now, *that's* more like it!" Jessica whispered to Elizabeth.

A beautiful tawny-haired woman in a forest-green silk dress was furiously typing on a computer. She glanced at the trio over the rims of her glasses. "Not now, Frank," she said, still typing.

"I'm not here to pester you for a date," Tony assured her, winking at Jessica and Elizabeth. "Orders from Henry. We have a couple of fresh new interns—twins, you see, a package deal—and he says we're to flip for them."

"We're working on the biggest murder in *years*, Frank, not to mention the missing princess," the woman reminded him crisply. "I don't have time to be a Girl Guides leader. They're all yours."

"Fair is fair," said Tony, taking a coin from his pocket. "Heads or tails?"

With an exasperated sigh, the woman pushed her glasses up on her nose. "Heads."

Tony flipped the coin, then showed her the results, a broad smile on his face. "What luck—heads it is! Elizabeth and Jessica Wakefield, meet your new boss, our distinguished crime editor, Lucy Friday."

Lucy narrowed her hazel eyes at Tony. *If looks could kill!* Elizabeth thought. Tony just grinned, his eyes fixed on Lucy's. Their staring contest lasted for a long, supercharged minute. Then, with another conspiratorial wink at the twins, Tony stuck his hands in his trouser pockets and sauntered off, whistling.

Surreptitiously, Jessica pinched Elizabeth's arm. The sisters were ecstatic. "We're going to cover the murder story with Lucy!" Jessica mouthed.

Lucy, meanwhile, was drumming her fingers on the desk. "I don't need a couple of interns tripping me up today," she grumbled. "You'll probably do fine on your own if the story's nothing too big. . . ."

She contemplated the storyboard, with its long list of crimes to be reported. Then she tore off a scrap of paper and scribbled rapidly. "Here," she said, handing the paper to Elizabeth along with two press cards she'd removed from her top desk drawer. "You'll cover Bumpo's beat. He's a Scotland Yard detective, and this morning he's looking into the case of Lady Wimpole's missing Yorkie. This is the address. Report back to me." With that, she turned back to her computer and resumed typing, apparently forgetting instantly that the twins even existed.

Press cards in hand, Jessica and Elizabeth headed out to the street. "A Scotland Yard detective!" Jessica gushed. "What's a Yorkie, anyway? A type of gemstone? A car?"

"A little yappie dog," her sister informed her flatly. "Our first crime story for the illustrious, high-toned *London Journal* is going to be about a lost *dog*!"

Jessica felt deflated, but only for a moment. "Let's make it fast, then," she recommended. "After Lady Wimpole's, we have to get to Essex Street."

"What's on Essex Street?" asked Elizabeth.

Jessica grinned triumphantly. "The scene of the crime—the big murder everybody's talking about. I saw the address written in Lois Lane's datebook."

Elizabeth grinned. "Very clever, little sister. Very clever!"

A maid in a crisp black uniform with a white apron and cap admitted them into Lady Wimpole's fashionable Knightsbridge townhouse. Stepping into the front parlor, Elizabeth and Jessica found the plump society matron seated on an overstuffed couch with a red-faced police detective, looking at photographs in a leather-bound album.

"And here's poor Poo-Poo on his third birthday," Lady Wimpole told the detective. Sniffling loudly, she dabbed her eyes with a lace-edged handkerchief. "We gave him the *loveliest* party. All the other doggies in the neighborhood were invited, and they brought the most generous, thoughtful gifts." She flipped to another page in the album. "And here is Poo-Poo at the seashore last holiday. Isn't he just darling in his little sunsuit?"

"Um, yes, yes, quite," Sergeant Bumpo mumbled, sliding a finger into his shirt collar as if it were choking him.

When Jessica and Elizabeth proffered their *Journal* press cards, Lady Wimpole beckoned them forward eagerly. "Oh, *do* write a thorough report, girls," she begged, "and see to it that it's featured prominently. Tell the editor I *insist*. We simply must find Poo-Poo—we *must*!"

Jessica put a hand to her mouth to smother a laugh. "Of course, of course. Ahem," Sergeant Bumpo spluttered. Patting his pockets for a minute or two, he finally located a small, dog-eared notebook and pencil. "Perhaps you could provide some details, Lady Wimpole," he requested, his expression remaining utterly serious. "When did your pet disappear and what were the circumstances?"

Their own pencils poised, Jessica and Elizabeth also waited politely for Lady Wimpole's response.

"It was last evening, at sunset," Lady Wimpole began, stifling a sob. "After supper, Grimsby, our butler, put Poo-Poo out as usual. But the careless man, not to notice that there was a hole in the garden fence!" Lady Wimpole's distress made her breathless; she gasped like a fish out of water.

"When Grimsby went to let Poo-Poo back in a quarter of an hour later, he was nowhere to be seen. Grimsby and Olivia the maid and Lord Wimpole traipsed up and down the street for *hours* calling Poo-Poo's name, but to no avail. I'm deathly afraid . . ." Lady Wimpole sank back against the sofa cushions, half fainting. "I'm *deathly* afraid it's the work of *dognappers*," she concluded in a weak but emphatic whisper.

"I see, I see." Sergeant Bumpo furrowed his brow and made a note of this theory. "Um, yes, hmm."

Jessica shot a mischievous glance at Elizabeth and then turned to the detective. "Dognappers," she mused, adopting a serious and professional air. "Has Cruella DeVille been rounded up for questioning, Sergeant?"

"DeVille, eh?" Elizabeth struggled not to laugh as Sergeant Bumpo put pencil to paper. "How did you spell that first name?"

As Jessica spelled the name of the villainess from *One Hundred and One Dalmations* for Sergeant Bumpo, Elizabeth turned away, trying to hide her laughter by pretending to be overcome by a fit of coughing.

"I think we have all the information we need for our story," Jessica declared, rising to her feet. "But do call us at the newspaper, Sergeant Bumpo, if you get any leads on the case."

"Oh, just one more thing," Lady Wimpole cried. Removing a photo from the album, she presented it to Elizabeth. "A picture of Poo-Poo to accompany your story." Her tiny eyes brimmed with tears. "And please mention that there will be a *sizable* reward to anyone who returns our darling to us."

Elizabeth pocketed the photograph. "We'll do that," she promised.

They left Sergeant Bumpo still in Lady Wimpole's clutches, squinting in a befuddled fashion at yet another doggie photo album. The maid showed them to the door. Safely outside on the sidewalk, Jessica and Elizabeth exploded with pent-up laughter.

"Oh, poor Lady Wimpole," Elizabeth gasped. "And poor Poo-Poo!"

"Dognapped—what a dire fate." Jessica clutched her sides. "Do you think Sergeant Bumpo will ever escape from that stuffy parlor?"

"At some point, Lady Wimpole has to let him go if she wants him to find her dog." Elizabeth wiped her eyes, hiccuping. "Fat chance of *that*, though. He couldn't find the notebook in his own pocket!"

"Obviously Scotland Yard gives him all the stupidest, most trivial cases. He couldn't be trusted to solve a *real* crime."

"Lucy probably thought she was keeping us out of trouble, assigning us to his beat," Elizabeth agreed.

"Lucky we know how to find action on our own!" Jessica pulled a London city map from her shoulder bag and quickly determined the quickest route to Essex Street. "There's the bus we want to take," she said, pointing to the corner. "Let's go!"

They got off at a bus stop half a block from the Essex Street address of the deceased Dr. Neville. Approaching the elegant Victorian-era townhouse, they saw signs of frantic activity in the otherwise quiet residential area. Sober-faced police officers bustled in and out of the building, which was cordoned off by bright yellow police tape; a stern-looking London bobby stood watchful guard at the wrought-iron gate.

Jessica and Elizabeth paused in the shadow of one of the spreading oaks that lined the street. "I don't know, Jess," Elizabeth said doubtfully. "How can we sneak past an entire *army* of police officers? I'm sure they won't want us snooping around!"

Jessica folded her arms across her chest and considered the situation. "We might as well try the oldest trick in the book," she said. "We've got nothing to lose if it doesn't work, right?"

Tiptoeing to the next tree, Jessica stooped and picked up a good-sized stone. Winding up like a major-league ball player, she pitched it as far as she could.

It hit the sidewalk twenty yards to the other side of Dr. Neville's gate. The bobby on guard heard the clatter; stepping onto the sidewalk to see what had caused the noise, he turned his back momentarily. Quick as a wink, the twins dashed from behind the tree and slipped through the open gate.

It was a short, tense sprint across the front

41

lawn. Diving into the cover of a rhododendron bush, Elizabeth and Jessica crouched close to the house, catching their breath and listening for sounds of pursuit. There were none.

"We made it!" Jessica whispered.

"Yeah, but now what?" Elizabeth wondered. "How do we get inside from here?"

"Maybe we don't need to go all the way inside," said Jessica. "I hear voices. There's a picture window above—let's just peek in."

Cautiously, the twins got to their feet again. The rhododendron continued to shield them, and they found that, when standing, their chins were just level with the windowsill and they could see inside. What they saw . . . and heard, however, almost made them wish they couldn't.

Elizabeth pressed a hand to her mouth, a tidal wave of nausea crashing over her. Then her journalistic instincts took over and, pulling her minicorder from her bag, she began describing what she saw.

The body of a man in dark flannel trousers and a camel's hair cardigan lay facedown in the middle of the parlor floor; underneath him, the pale carpet was soaked with blood.

"It's him," Jessica gasped excitedly. "It's the dead man!"

Lucy Friday stood close to the corpse, looking down at it and reciting something into a hand-held tape recorder similar to Elizabeth's. A flashbulb popped as a police photographer snapped shots of the body from various angles.

"Who do you suppose *they* are?" Elizabeth whispered to Jessica. There were two other people in the room, both well-dressed, middle-aged men. "They don't look like police."

"Private detectives? Friends of the doctor? The guy on the left looks pretty upset." Raising her camera, Jessica took a quick picture of the scene through the glass. "What's that thing he's holding?"

The man was staring down in disbelief at something flat and silver lying in the palm of his hand. "A cigarette case, maybe," Elizabeth guessed.

The side window was open a crack, and at that moment Lucy Friday's clear, dispassionate voice drifted out to them. The sight of the body was horrible enough, but her words were even more disturbing—they chilled Jessica and Elizabeth to the very bone. "The victim's throat has been ripped open," Lucy recorded, "as if by a wild beast. . . ."

Chapter 4

Five minutes later, Elizabeth and Jessica were riding a red double-decker bus back toward the *Journal*. Elizabeth sat with her shoulders hunched, still tense with dread; Jessica slumped, drained as if she'd just run a marathon.

"I think we got more than we bargained for when we set out looking for an exciting story," Jessica whispered.

Elizabeth nodded, shivering. Jessica's words on the airplane and Lucy Friday's observation over the body echoed through her brain. *I wouldn't mind a nice, ghoulish London murder. . . . The victim's throat has been ripped out, as if by a wild beast. . . .*

The twins relaxed somewhat as the bus carried them farther and farther from the scene of the crime. Still, when their stop approached and they stood to walk to the front of the bus, Elizabeth realized her knees were still shaking.

It was a sunny day, and the busy city seemed vibrantly alive—a stark contrast, Elizabeth couldn't help thinking, to the lifeless corpse in the dim parlor. As she jumped onto the sidewalk, she took a deep breath of fresh air, willing herself to feel a renewed sense of courage. *You're supposed to be a crime reporter,* she reminded herself, *cool and collected like Lucy Friday.*

"That was totally gruesome," Jessica said with relish as they trotted up the stairs to the *London Journal's* revolving doors. Having put a safe distance between herself and the dead body, Jessica had brightened up considerably. "Too bad Lucy would probably fire us if she found out we snuck over to Dr. Neville's." She patted her shoulder bag with the camera inside. "It would be so cool to write this up as our first article for the *Journal*—we have pictures and everything!"

Elizabeth didn't even like to think about that roll of film. "Just don't let anything slip to Lucy," she advised. "We were at Lady Wimpole's this whole time, OK?"

"Gotcha," said Jessica.

When they reported to Lucy's desk a few minutes later, they found the crime editor taking off her jacket and hanging it on the back of her chair. *She just got back from Dr. Neville's herself,* Elizabeth speculated, shooting a glance at Jessica.

"We got the story from Lady Wimpole," Jessica said. "What would you like us to do now?"

"Lady Wimpole?" Dropping a stack of folders and her datebook on the desk, Lucy blinked distractedly at Jessica. "Oh, right—the dog. Well, let's see. Why doesn't one of you write a blurb for this evening's 'Crime Reporter' column?"

"I'll do that," Elizabeth volunteered.

"Here's yesterday's paper. 'Crime Reporter' is at the back of the second section—take a look at how we present the short pieces," Lucy recommended. "As for you, Jessica . . ." She checked the story-board once more. Quite a few items had been checked off as reporters divvied up the prospects and headed out to research their stories. Lucy's lips twitched, as if she were trying not to smile. "How about another Bumpo case? He's scheduled to look into a problem at Pembroke Green this after-noon—a theft of some sort. Get a write-up to me by four and we can squeeze that in tonight's 'Crime Reporter,' too."

Jessica rolled her eyes. "Not Bumpo again!" she groaned to Elizabeth as soon as they were out of earshot.

"Would you rather write up the Poo-Poo Report?" Elizabeth asked.

The two giggled. "I guess not." Jessica grinned. "If the rest of the Sweet Valley High newspaper staff could see you now!"

Tucked away in the remote corner of the office where Tony Frank had located a vacant desk for her, Elizabeth typed a few more words. She had nearly finished the Poo-Poo story, but it had taken much longer than it should have. She just couldn't concentrate. The report was fairly straightforward, but her thoughts kept drifting . . . back to Essex Street and the horrible fate of the unfortunate Dr. Neville.

Rewinding her mini-corder, Elizabeth played back the last part of the tape. As she listened to her own frightened whisper, a chill raced up her spine, making her teeth chatter. *The poor man's throat was ripped out,* Elizabeth thought, hugging herself to stop from shaking. Along with distress and revulsion, she couldn't help feeling curiosity, too. Who would commit such a vile crime, and why? What kind of person had Dr. Neville been; did he have enemies? Who were the two men standing over the body with Lucy?

Elizabeth hit the off button on the mini-corder just as someone spoke behind her. "Excuse me," a voice said timidly.

Elizabeth jumped, her heart leaping into her throat. Swiveling, she found herself face-to-face with the handsome, dark-haired boy she'd seen earlier that day, the one who'd run away when she tried to talk to him.

The boy tossed hair back from his forehead and gave her a rueful smile. "I came to apologize for being impolite this morning—and, look, now I've practically scared you to death," he said in a lilting, adorable English accent. "You'll have to forgive me twice over now. This morning, I was just so absorbed in my writing that you took me by surprise." His smile deepened, making his eyes crinkle at the corners. "I felt guilty, you see. Caught in the act." Leaning closer, he confided, "I was writing poems instead of working on my newspaper story."

Elizabeth couldn't tell him why she'd been so jumpy, so instead she stood up and extended a hand. "I'm Elizabeth Wakefield," she told him. "My twin sister, Jessica, and I are summer interns, from the States."

"Luke Shepherd." He gave her hand a light squeeze. "It's a pleasure to meet you."

"And to meet you." For some reason, Elizabeth felt herself blushing; maybe it was Luke's touch, or the shyly admiring look in his intensely blue eyes. She dropped her gaze. "Well . . ."

"I say, Elizabeth." Luke glanced at his watch. "Would you let me take you out to tea, to make up for my rudeness? I know a place just a few blocks away where the sandwiches are as thick as your arm and the Devonshire cream is the sweetest you'll find anywhere in London."

Elizabeth glanced down at her not-quite-finished report. Bending, she quickly keyed in a concluding sentence and then pressed the print command. "Let me just turn this in to my boss," she told Luke after the printer had spit it out. "If she gives me permission to leave early, I'd love to have tea with you."

"Pembroke Green," Jessica murmured to herself. The Pembroke family's stately residence, situated on one of the most fashionable squares in town, was encircled by lush gardens. "I see where it gets its name."

49

A minute after she rang the bell, the door was opened by a uniformed maid who might have been the twin of Lady Wimpole's. Jessica exhibited her press card. "I'm here to ask Lady Pembroke a few questions about the theft," she said in her most serious and self-important manner.

The maid led her to the rear of the house. Green filtered sunlight poured into the large, airy drawing room from an attached solarium filled with potted plants.

Sergeant Bumpo was standing awkwardly at attention in front of a regally seated Lady Pembroke. The thin, jewelry-bedecked woman, who was coiffed and manicured within an inch of her life, didn't bother rising when Jessica entered the room. "It's about time," Lady Pembroke said somewhat peevishly. "I certainly hope my story will be included in the P.M. edition. People should be *warned* what can happen when they check their furs at Brown's!"

What is she talking about? Jessica wondered. "I need you to start at the beginning," she requested, perching gingerly on the edge of a brocade-upholstered wing chair, even though Lady Pembroke hadn't invited her to sit down. Taking out her notebook, she tried her best to look professional. "What was stolen, and where did the theft occur?"

Lady Pembroke heaved an impatient sigh. "I was just telling the Sergeant, but I *suppose* I can go over it again. I was having tea at Brown's Hotel yesterday afternoon, and I made the mistake of checking my new mink."

Jessica bit her tongue to keep from saying, *You were wearing a* mink *in the* summer?

"Imagine my dismay when I claimed it," Lady Pembroke continued, "and wound up with a wretched chinchilla instead!"

"Wretched chinchilla," Jessica repeated, dutifully making a note.

"There it is, over there." Lady Pembroke waved a languid hand across the room at something brown and furry lying on the piano bench.

"Ah ha," grunted Sergeant Bumpo. Eager to examine the evidence, he hurried over to the piano, catching a toe under the edge of the Oriental rug as he went, nearly falling flat on his face.

Jessica swallowed a giggle. "Did you point out the mistake right away, or didn't you notice until you got home?" she asked.

Lady Pembroke arched an overplucked eyebrow. "Of course I realized *instantly* that I'd been given the wrong fur. But the scatterbrained coat-check girl insisted that I'd checked the chinchilla. I demanded that the maître d' intercede and he searched high and low, but my mink had vanished. The dismal, stupid girl had sent it home with someone else!"

"How upsetting that must have been for you," Jessica murmured. *Especially as you probably have a whole closetful of minks upstairs!*

"Oh, it was." Lady Pembroke sighed. "It was."

At that moment, a movement in the hallway caught Jessica's attention. She turned her head just as a remarkably handsome young man in formal

English riding gear passed by the entrance to the drawing room. *Wow!* Straining to get a better look at him, Jessica nearly fell off her chair. *Yoo-hoo, over here!*

To her profound disappointment, the debonair young man didn't enter the sitting room, but rather turned on his boot heel to exchange a few words with another man who'd just entered behind him. The second man was quite a bit older, but there was a distinct family resemblance. *Father and son,* Jessica guessed. *Lord Pembroke, a.k.a. Mr. Wretched Chinchilla, and Lord Pembroke Junior.* Then something about the older man triggered Jessica's memory. *It's the man with the cigarette case!* she realized with a jolt of excited recognition. *The one who was standing over Dr. Neville's body!*

The two men moved out of sight, and Jessica did her best to refocus on Lady Pembroke and Sergeant Bumpo. Wrinkling his nose distastefully, the detective held the chinchilla at arm's length as if it were still alive and might bite him.

Jessica sneezed to disguise the laughter bubbling up in her throat. "Achew!"

"Bless you," Bumpo said solemnly. Then he turned to Lady Pembroke, clicking his heels together. "I'll need to confiscate this."

"By all means, take it—take it out of my sight."

"Is there anything else you think I should know?" Jessica asked Lady Pembroke, looking for a way to prolong the interview so she might get another glimpse of the handsome horseman.

"That's all, I believe," Lady Pembroke replied.

52

"Well, let's just go over this one last time," Jessica suggested. "I want to be sure the story is accurate in every detail."

With painstaking slowness, Jessica read back her notes to Lady Pembroke, keeping one eye on the hallway. Sergeant Bumpo, meanwhile, continued to prowl around the drawing room, occasionally colliding with something; a Ming vase came perilously near to sliding off a shelf and a fragile lamp teetered precariously.

Finally, there was nothing left for Jessica to do but tuck her notebook back in her shoulder bag. "Thanks for your cooperation," she said to Lady Pembroke. "I hope you get your mink back."

"Never fear," proclaimed Sergeant Bumpo.

"Well . . . so long." Jessica stood up just as the young man she'd spotted earlier strode into the room. Having showered and shaved, he now wore the clothes of an English gentleman, ascot and all. *He can't be real,* Jessica thought. *I must have wandered onto a movie set!*

The young man directed an amused glance at Sergeant Bumpo and then fixed a pair of dazzling midnight-blue eyes on Jessica. The frank admiration she saw there made her heart somersault.

"Exercising your power over the minions again, eh, Mother?" the young man teased. He continued to gaze at Jessica, his chiseled, aristocratic lips curling in a smile. "I'm Lady Pembroke's son, little Lord Pembroke. But you can call me Robert. And I can call you . . . ?"

Anytime! Jessica thought. "Jessica Wakefield,"

she said breathlessly. "From the *London Journal*."

"The *Journal*—yes, of course." Still smiling, Robert gave her a quick, practiced look up and down. "A bit young to be a reporter, aren't you? And if I'm not mistaken, your accent is distinctly American."

Jessica conceded the American part but hedged about her age in case Robert, who appeared to be about twenty, might lose interest if he knew she was only sixteen. "I'm a summer intern from the States. This is my first day on the job."

"And what an exciting day it's been, eh?" he kidded. "Somebody made off with Mother's mink. What's the world coming to?"

"Oh, Robert," Lady Pembroke said with mock exasperation. "Must you be flip about absolutely everything?"

"I'm not flip, I'm deadly serious," he swore. "So serious that I intend to do some of my own investigating. Have you gotten all the pertinent details, Miss Wakefield?"

When Jessica nodded, Robert took her left hand and hooked it through his arm. "Then how about tea at Brown's?" he suggested in the brash, confident manner of someone used to having his every wish gratified. He winked rakishly at Lady Pembroke. "There's no substitute for a visit to the scene of the crime, wouldn't you say, Mother?"

Luke opened the door to the pub. "The Slaughtered Lamb's not fancy, but the grub's first-rate," he promised.

Before stepping into the dark, wood-smoky interior, Elizabeth glanced up at the old wooden sign. It depicted a wolf standing over the body of a dead lamb, blood dripping from his fangs. "What a creepy name, though," she said. "And it was the name of the pub in this really scary movie I just saw, *An American Werewolf in London*. Did you ever see it?"

Luke's lips curved in a smile. "I did, as a matter of fact. Several times. But this is a different kind of pub, on my honor. Warm and cozy. You'll like it."

As they slid into a booth near the stone fireplace, Elizabeth smiled at Luke. "You're right, it is different. I like it already."

"It's the real thing. Not many pubs like this left in the city nowadays." He smiled wryly. "They've all given way to American fast-food restaurants."

Elizabeth laughed. "Don't blame me! I'm American, but I'd rather eat someplace like this anyday."

They ordered sandwiches, scones, and a pot of tea, and then a shy silence descended over them. "So . . ." Luke looked down at his hands, folded on top of the table, and then up at Elizabeth. "You and your sister are from California, ay? Just here for the summer?"

"Sweet Valley, California," said Elizabeth. "On the coast, north of L.A."

"Sweet Valley." A smile touched Luke's lips. "Sounds like heaven."

"It's beautiful," Elizabeth had to admit. "But we couldn't wait to come to London. This is such an exciting city, and there's so much *history*."

"Where are you staying?"

"HIS—Housing for International Students. It's like a dorm, with kids from all over the world."

The waitress placed a pot of steaming tea, cream and sugar, and two mugs on the table. "What do you think of the *Journal* so far?" asked Luke, pouring Elizabeth a mug of tea.

Tipping her head to one side, Elizabeth decided to be honest. Her instincts told her she could count on Luke's sympathy. "I was a little disappointed—no, a *lot* disappointed!—that Mr. Reeves basically forgot we were coming. But I know he's really busy, and it will probably work out fine. He turned us over to Tony Frank, who turned us over to Lucy Friday, who turned us over to Sergeant Bumpo of Scotland Yard."

"Scotland Yard—that sounds promising."

Elizabeth grinned. "Yeah. We reported on an investigation into a big disappearance."

"The princess?" guessed Luke.

"No, Poo-Poo the Yorkshire Terrier." Elizabeth related the episode at Lady Wimpole's, taking pleasure in Luke's hearty laughter. "Yes, you could say we're on the fast track. But what about you? What's your position at the *Journal*?"

A platter of sandwiches and scones was deposited on the table. After offering them to Elizabeth, Luke selected a fat, buttery scone, fresh from the oven. "I'm fairly new at the paper myself," he said, splitting the scone and spreading it with thick Devonshire cream. "I write for the arts

56

and literature section, film and book reviews mostly. I'm hoping I'll have time to keep up with it when I start at the university in the fall—the cash would come in handy."

"And you write poems, too," said Elizabeth, topping her own scone with a dollop of strawberry jam.

"Yes. Just for myself, of course. As I said, that's what I was doing when you came upon me this morning. Sometimes the inspiration just strikes . . . there's nothing I can do but give in to it." His face reddened. "It probably sounds silly to you."

"Oh, not at all." Elizabeth reached out impulsively to touch his hand, her eyes shining. "I understand perfectly. I have a notebook, too, where I keep my journal, and I wouldn't go anywhere without it. I love poetry—it's my favorite thing."

Their eyes locked and a warm current of sympathy coursed between them, binding them close. "Thanks for not making fun of me," Luke said softly.

"I wouldn't, ever," Elizabeth replied.

Another spell of silence followed, but this time it was comfortable. Though she still didn't know much about him, Luke had ceased to be a stranger to Elizabeth, and she could tell he felt the same way about her.

Finishing her first scone, Elizabeth reached for another. "Did you move to London when you got the job at the *Journal*, or does your family live here?" she asked.

"My family . . ." Luke toyed with his teaspoon.

"My father is my only family. My father, and Mrs. Weldon, our housekeeper. We live in a house on the outskirts of town. A nice enough old house—I was born there, and so was my dad—but in desperate need of a new coat of paint, I'm sorry to say. My mother . . ." Luke's eyes dropped and Elizabeth saw his jaw clench. "My mother died of pneumonia when I was a boy."

"I'm sorry," Elizabeth whispered. "Oh, that must have been so hard."

When Luke looked up at Elizabeth, his eyes were damp with unshed tears. "I was very close to her—she was my whole world."

He pulled his wallet from his trouser pocket and removed a faded, creased photograph. Wordlessly, he handed the picture to Elizabeth. The lovely young woman looked very much like Luke. She had the same sweep of raven hair, the same spectacular blue eyes, the same shy, warm smile. "She's beautiful," said Elizabeth.

"She was even more beautiful on the inside," said Luke. "She was smart and kind. She was a writer, too—in fact, she staffed for the *London Journal* for a time. Working there . . ." Luke's voice cracked with emotion. "I feel painfully close to her."

Sympathetic tears sparkled in Elizabeth's eyes. "I can imagine." She shifted the subject somewhat, hoping to cheer Luke up. "How about your father—is he also a writer?"

Instantly, the sorrow on Luke's face gave way to a look of disdain. "My father doesn't have an ounce of creativity in his bones. He runs a shabby little corner drugstore—he's a pharmacist."

Luke's sudden hostility took Elizabeth by surprise. "Well . . ." she murmured awkwardly.

Luke studied her face. "I know what you're thinking. Such a tragedy *could* have brought my father and me closer together. Maybe if he'd shown some emotion when she died . . . but he didn't even seem to feel it. And when she fell sick, he should have known." Luke's hand tightened around the mug of tea, his knuckles whitening. "Of all people, as a druggist, he should have known how serious it was, how quickly pneumonia can take a turn for the worse and be fatal."

Luke shook his head. "I guess there are times when, even after all these years, I still can't believe she's gone. Forgive me for getting so emotional. And for talking so much about myself! I hope I haven't scared you off." His manner brightened; he smiled. "Because I want to learn about *you*, Elizabeth, and about life in the United States. Do you have any other brothers or sisters? What is your school like? Do you belong to clubs and play sports?"

Luke listened with an animated expression as Elizabeth told stories about her family and Sweet Valley. He prompted her with questions, as if hungry for conversation. *He's lonely,* Elizabeth sensed. *He must not have many people to talk to—he's eager for us to be friends.*

That was fine with her. She was incredibly glad she'd bumped into Luke on her first day working at the *Journal*. He'd struck a chord deep inside her. She felt tremendous compassion—and attraction—for this solitary, motherless poet.

"Another cup of tea, Jessica?"

Jessica nodded. "That would be lovely."

Robert lifted his chin and a waiter came running to ascertain his wishes. Within moments, their delicate china cups were refilled with hot tea and their plates with a fresh assortment of exquisite little cakes and tiny sandwiches.

This is the life, Jessica thought, gazing at her companion with something like awe. *Robert Pembroke, you are the man of my dreams!*

It was almost too good to be true. Here she was, sipping fragrant tea at the poshest hotel in London with the suave and handsome Lord Robert Pembroke, whom she'd met only an hour before. And *everyone* seemed to recognize him. It was such a thrill, being the object of admiring, envious glances—Jessica felt like a movie star.

Robert resumed the story he'd been telling, with a smitten Jessica hanging on his every word. "It really wasn't so bad, getting kicked out of Eaton," he drawled. "My parents just packed me off to auntie's for the summer. They thought perhaps my cousin would be a good influence on me. My cousin . . . Prince Malcolm," he added casually.

Jessica's jaw dropped. "*The* Prince Malcolm?"

"None other," said Robert.

"So, 'auntie' is . . ."

"The queen," he confirmed.

Jessica's already high opinion of Robert

Pembroke now soared up into the stratosphere. "You're *related* to the royal family?" she squeaked. "They're your *cousins*?"

"Well, it's a rather distant connection," he admitted. "Third cousins, once removed—something like that. But we've always been quite close."

Jessica tried to keep a grip on what was left of her composure; it was hard not to come across as a total starstruck idiot. "Umm," she murmured encouragingly, hoping to hear juicy details about his royal relations—maybe even get the inside scoop on the disappearance of Princess Eliana.

"But what about *you*, Jessica?" Robert leaned forward, his foot brushing hers under the table. "How do you come to be working for my father's newspaper?"

"Your father's newspaper?" Jessica echoed, worrying that she was starting to sound like a parrot.

"My humble clan owns the *London Journal*, didn't you know that?" Robert grinned wickedly. "Why do you suppose you got exclusive rights to Mummy's tragic tale?"

Jessica laughed. "It was the first story I've investigated on my very own. It could be my big breakthrough, the stepping-stone to my own byline."

Robert patted the pockets of his jacket. "Now, where are my cigarettes? Just as well I haven't got them—I really should kick the habit. So, you want to be a journalist, Jessica."

"Not really," she admitted. "My sister does— I'm mostly along for the ride."

"And how's the . . . ride . . . so far?"

Jessica dimpled flirtatiously. "We only arrived yesterday, but already I have a feeling it's going to be the ride of my life."

"We'll make sure of it," Robert declared. "You know, my father takes quite an active interest in the paper, and he's always hoped I'd follow his example, take over the reins someday. Can't say I've lived up to his expectations . . . although I did stop in last week to hobnob a bit with ol' Henry. He seemed to be frantically worried about the *London Daily Post* stealing away our readers. Not bloody likely if you ask me. But now . . ." The look Robert gave her made Jessica's heart melt like butter. "It appears that I'll have to find more excuses to drop by the office. In the meantime . . ." Reaching across the table, he touched her hand. "Are you free tomorrow evening? May I show you around my city?"

Jessica forced herself to take a sip of tea before replying. She didn't want to come across as too eager, to reveal that she was totally infatuated. Rich, handsome, elegant, sophisticated Lord Robert Pembroke had taken her out to tea, and she'd obviously passed muster because now he was asking her for a *real* date!

"I'd love that," she said casually, thinking meanwhile, *If Lila and Amy could see me now!*

Chapter 5

Elizabeth was sitting with her legs hooked over the arm of an easy chair, her eyes half closed and a dreamy smile on her lips, when Jessica burst into their room at HIS just before dinnertime.

"You won't believe what happened to me this afternoon." Tossing her shoulder bag onto the bed, Jessica flung herself into the other chair. "You won't *believe* who I've fallen madly in love with!"

Elizabeth opened her eyes and fixed her sister with a mischievous smile. "Sergeant Bumpo?"

"Actually, that imbecile played cupid, in a manner of speaking. If Lucy hadn't assigned us to his beat, I wouldn't have gone to Pembroke Green on a story. And if I hadn't gone to Pembroke Green, I wouldn't have met Lord Pembroke Junior, and if I hadn't met Lord Pembroke Junior, he couldn't have taken me out to tea at Brown's Hotel!"

"Lord Pembroke Junior took you out to tea at

Brown's Hotel?" repeated Elizabeth. "Who's he? Where's that?"

"Liz, you wouldn't believe their house, and it's just their *London* residence—they have a castle in the country. A castle, a real live castle! And not only *that*." Jessica paused dramatically. "They're related to the *queen*. The queen! Robert practically grew up in Buckingham Palace, playing cricket and polo and what have you with Prince Malcolm."

"Wow," Elizabeth said politely.

"I'll never be able to date a Sweet Valley High boy again," Jessica concluded with a rapturous sigh. "Now that I know what it's like to go out with a *nobleman*."

Elizabeth smiled. "I had a feeling it wouldn't take you long to elbow your way into the royal family."

"I didn't elbow my way anywhere," Jessica insisted righteously. "Can I help it if Robert Pembroke took one look at me and fell head over heels for my sexy American style?"

Her sister laughed. "I guess not."

"So what about you?" Jessica kicked off her shoes and tucked her legs up on the chair. "How did you spend *your* afternoon?"

Elizabeth glanced out the window, the dreamy look returning to her eyes. "I went out to tea with a guy from work," she replied. "Luke Shepherd. He writes for the arts and literature section—I'll introduce you to him tomorrow."

"I don't suppose *he's* related to royalty," said Jessica with a superior sniff.

Elizabeth shook her head. "No, but he's very

nice. And smart and sensitive. . . . We had the most interesting talk! It was as if we'd known each other for years instead of hours." Her cheeks warmed, remembering the intimacy of their booth at the Slaughtered Lamb. "After tea, he took me for a walking tour of literary London. It was wonderful, like stepping back in time." Her eyes sparkled with animation. "We saw places that Dickens and Trollope and Thackeray wrote about, and where E. M. Forster and Virginia Woolf and the rest of the Bloomsbury group lived, and where Henry James went for tea and an afternoon stroll. Luke's read more books than anyone I've ever met, including Mr. Collins. He's so different from . . ."

The sentence trailed off, unfinished. Elizabeth's blush deepened. *What am I doing, comparing Todd to Luke?* she wondered with a pang of guilt.

Elizabeth knew she should be pining for her boyfriend, but it was useless to pretend that Luke Shepherd hadn't made a striking impression on her. She shrugged, trying to sound more casual. "There's just . . . something about him."

"Yeah, something incredibly *boring*," Jessica remarked, yawning. "A walking tour of literary London—blech. You have a warped idea of fun, Liz."

"To each her own, I guess."

"You'd better believe it. Lord Pembroke's taking me out tomorrow night and, I can tell you, *we* won't be *walking* anywhere. It's going to be limousines all the way!"

"Well, la di da. Excuse *me*, Lady Robert Pembroke *Junior*."

"Lady Pembroke—I like the sound of *that*. Am I glad I didn't decide to settle for one of these run-of-the-mill HIS boys."

Luke's pale, romantic face faded from Elizabeth's mind, and the bronzed, chiseled features of Rene Glize took its place. "I almost forgot about Rene," she mused out loud. "We never really got to explore our feelings for each other in France."

"Well, if you want my opinion," said Jessica, "this Luke guy sounds like a dud. Rene, on the other hand, is a total— Hey, what's that on your bed?"

Elizabeth hadn't noticed it before, but now she saw that someone had placed a red rose on her pillow. Padding over, she picked up the rose and the folded note that lay beneath it. "It's from Rene," she told Jessica.

"Read it, read it!" Jessica clamored.

"'*Chere* Elizabeth, I'll be at an embassy function all evening, but didn't want to waste a minute making a date with you. Would you have dinner with me tomorrow night? I know a wonderful little French café. . . . I hope you are free tomorrow, as it's my only night off all week and I want to spend it with you. Please leave me a note. Love, Rene.'"

"Ooh la la," Jessica teased, pursing her lips and blowing a noisy kiss. "Sounds like Rene's ready to explore *his* feelings."

Elizabeth blushed more furiously than ever. "I'm sure we both want the same thing—to be very good friends. Unlike *some* people, I didn't come to London looking for romance."

Jessica shook her head. "Still . . . two new suitors in twenty-four hours, Liz?" she teased. "I'd say that's moving pretty fast for somebody who's not looking for romance. Poor, poor Todd!"

I didn't come to London to look for romance, Elizabeth repeated to herself as she scribbled a note to Rene, accepting his invitation to dinner the following night. An image flickered through her mind—a boy's lake-blue eyes, milky skin, and sweep of dark hair. . . .

Quickly, Elizabeth banished the picture of Luke Shepherd, summoning up instead Todd's warm smile and coffee-brown eyes. "Are you ready?" Jessica asked impatiently.

Folding the note, Elizabeth followed her sister out of the bedroom. As they walked downstairs, she glanced at her watch. "Dinner doesn't start for five minutes," she said. "Let's run out and buy the evening edition of the *Journal*."

"I can't wait to see my story about Lady Pembroke's mink. If it's not on the front page, I'm quitting," Jessica joked.

"You know what *will* be on the front page—Dr. Neville's murder," Elizabeth reminded her.

"I almost forgot about that. This was such a long day. It feels like years since we looked in the window and saw . . . *him*."

Elizabeth shivered. *I'll never forget,* she thought. *The body, the blood . . .*

"C'mon." Jessica pushed open the door to the street. "Or we'll be the last ones into dinner and we'll get stuck sitting with Portia."

They jogged to the nearest newsstand, three blocks away near the tube entrance. Fishing in her purse for change, Elizabeth paid the vendor while Jessica picked up a copy of the *Journal*.

Side by side, they peered eagerly at the headlines. "Where's the murder story?" Jessica asked.

Elizabeth's eyes ran up and down the front page. "I don't see it," she said, surprised. "Maybe it's on the second page."

Jessica snatched the paper from her. "Let's find our stories first. Lucy said 'Crime Reporter' is at the back of the second section."

Sure enough, half of the second-to-last page of the local news section was devoted to the London 'Crime Reporter,' edited by Lucy Friday. "Look!" Jessica squealed, delighted. "There's my piece, 'The Fur Flies at Brown's.' Doesn't it look great?"

"Great title." Elizabeth found her own piece sandwiched between write-ups about a downtown traffic accident and a foiled bank robbery. "No picture of Poo-Poo—Lady Wimpole will be disappointed!"

"Liz, look." Jessica pointed to a box set next to the 'Crime Reporter' column. "The Dr. Neville murder story!"

It took only a moment to skim the article, which wasn't much longer than the 'Crime Reporter' blurbs. "What's a big story like this doing buried back here?" wondered Jessica.

A puzzled frown creased Elizabeth's forehead. "It's not a big story anymore. Listen to this: 'Prominent physician Cameron Neville was killed in his home late Sunday night. He was pronounced dead on the scene by London Police Department emergency medics. Memorial services will be held . . . ' Et cetera."

"They left out all the gory details!" Jessica cried.

"You can't even tell from this that he was *murdered* as opposed to being killed accidentally," Elizabeth agreed.

"People don't get their throats ripped out by accident," Jessica declared. "It's not like falling down the stairs or something. I don't get it. After all the fuss everyone was making, why would Lucy play down the story like this?"

Elizabeth chewed her lip. "She wouldn't. This can't be the article she was working on all day. It simply can't be."

Thoughtfully, she turned back to the front page. "Maybe that's why Dr. Neville got shoved to the back of the paper," Jessica speculated. "The missing princess is still hogging all the headlines." She indicated the biggest one. "'Princess Eliana Kidnapped?' Wow, that's terrible! Did they get a ransom note? Who did it?"

Elizabeth ran her eye down the column of print. "According to this, there hasn't actually been a ransom note. They don't have *evidence* that she was kidnapped—it's just a theory."

"So, that huge headline's just to catch people's eyes and sell more papers."

"I guess so. I didn't think the *Journal* stooped to sensationalism—I thought it was intellectual and objective."

Jessica shrugged. "It's a big story—you can't blame them for playing it for everything it's worth."

"Then why wouldn't they do the same with Dr. Neville's murder?" Elizabeth countered. "What could be more sensational than that?"

"Good point."

For a minute, the sisters stood reading the paper in silence. Accompanying the story about Princess Eliana was an interview with Andrew Thatcher, the London chief of police. Suddenly, Elizabeth's eyes widened in startled recognition. "This man!" she gasped, pointing to the photograph of the police chief. "Jessica, wasn't he . . . ?"

Jessica studied the picture and then nodded excitedly. "The other man we saw through the window at Dr. Neville's!"

Elizabeth blinked at her sister. "The *other* man?"

"Didn't I tell you?" Jessica slapped the palm of her hand to her forehead. "I can't believe I forgot—I guess I was so wrapped up in Robert that I—Lord Pembroke!" she explained disjointedly. "Or rather, Lord Pembroke *Senior*. Robert's father. I caught a glimpse of him at Pembroke Green and I'm ninety-nine percent positive he was one of the two men standing over the body, the one holding the cigarette case."

"And the London chief of police was the other," Elizabeth mused. "Lord Pembroke Senior . . . hmm. Do you suppose he was a friend of Dr. Neville, or a patient? Or could he have been there just by coincidence?"

"I have no idea," said Jessica. "I didn't think to ask Robert about it."

"It's better that you didn't, since we weren't supposed to be spying through that window in the first place. Officially, we don't know anything."

"Unofficially, we don't know anything, either," Jessica pointed out. "Lord Pembroke Senior and Police Chief Thatcher were at Dr. Neville's, but so what?"

"It may mean something," Elizabeth insisted. "It *has* to mean something. If the chief of police himself went to investigate Dr. Neville's death, then it must be a high-profile crime, so why wasn't it given bigger press?"

"Something's fishy," Jessica concluded.

"Something's *very* fishy," Elizabeth agreed.

"Well, take your pick," Jessica whispered in Elizabeth's ear as they stood in the entrance to the HIS dining room five minutes later. "There are two free seats at that table . . . and a few more over there."

Elizabeth stifled a giggle as she surveyed their choices. Lina, Emily, David, and Gabriello sat at a table for six near the big bay window, while a solitary Portia occupied a small table in the corner, the book in her free hand held to eye level as if to block out any offensive view of her dormmates.

The twins made a beeline for the group by the window. "Hi, everybody!" Jessica said brightly, slipping into an empty chair.

She tossed the folded newspaper onto the

table, front page up. Lina jumped.

"Not more missing princess headlines," Emily groaned, seizing the paper and throwing it under the table. "Does anyone mind if we *don't* spend the entire meal discussing who might have kidnapped her?"

"Fine with me," said Gabriello, tearing off a hunk of fresh-baked bread and then passing the loaf to Elizabeth.

"And me," murmured Lina.

"Tell us about your first day at the *Journal*," invited Emily as the kitchen staff began distributing plates piled high with pot roast, peas, and potatoes. "Did you get a good assignment or is it going to be deadly dull?"

Elizabeth shot a glance at Jessica, knowing her sister had the same thought. *Deadly yes, but not dull!*

"We're covering the beat of a Scotland Yard detective who couldn't solve a crime if it happened right under his nose," Jessica told Emily and the others. "Sergeant Bumpo."

David chuckled. "Is that really his name?"

Jessica nodded. "And it suits him perfectly. He's like a bull in a china shop—he crashed into just about every breakable thing in the drawing room at Pembroke Green. Which reminds me!" she exclaimed, turning to Emily with sparkling eyes. "Guess who's taking me out on the town tomorrow night?"

Emily laughed. "Don't tell me you've already met Prince Charming!"

"*Lord* Charming, actually," said Jessica, dimpling. "Robert, the only son of Lord and Lady Pembroke of Pembroke Green and Pembroke Manor."

"The Pembrokes own half of England, and the *London Journal* to boot!" Emily cried.

Elizabeth's eyebrows arched in surprise. "They own the *Journal*?"

Jessica nodded. "Isn't it exciting, Em?"

"You're the luckiest girl in the world," her friend declared. "Now if some of your luck would only rub off on me . . . !"

As Emily begged Jessica for a blow-by-blow account of tea with Robert Pembroke, Elizabeth smiled at Lina. "How was *your* day?"

Lina pushed a strand of hair back from her forehead and smiled back wearily. "Long. Tiring. But we fed forty people, found an apartment for a family of five, and helped a dozen or so fill out job applications. Sometimes I see the faintest glimmer of light at the end of the tunnel."

"You know, Lina, I . . . um, I think what you're doing is very admirable," a male voice ventured hesitantly.

Elizabeth and Lina both turned to look at the speaker. David ducked his head, hiding his eyes behind a shock of hair. "I know what it's like to go without, that's all," he continued, speaking down to his plate. "You're good to help them who are hard up."

Now it was Lina's turn to drop her gaze and blush. "It's nothing," she mumbled.

It was the first time Elizabeth had heard quiet

73

David Bartholomew utter two sentences in a row, and she waited with interest, hoping he'd pursue the conversation. Instead, he retreated back into his shell. Lina, too, fell silent, eating methodically with her eyes downcast. *Either she hasn't noticed that David has a huge crush on her,* Elizabeth mused, *or she doesn't want to notice.*

Jessica had finished reenacting every look and word that had passed between her and Robert Pembroke, and now she heaved a grumpy sigh. "This curfew is really going to cramp my style," she complained. "How am I going to tell Robert that Mrs. Bates will have my hide if I'm not back by eleven?"

"It's a total drag," agreed Gabriello. "A friend of mine from the music department at the university plays bass for a rock band, Lunar Landscape. They're booked at Mondo tonight and I'd love to go hear them, but the show doesn't even *start* until eleven."

"Mondo," Jessica raved. "Robert says that's the hippest club in London right now!"

"Robert's right," confirmed Gabriello. "So, what do you say we all sneak out after curfew and go dancing?"

Elizabeth could tell he was just kidding, but to her surprise Lina, of all people, took the suggestion at face value. "Let's do it! I haven't been to Mondo in the longest—" She checked herself. "I mean, I'd really like to hear some live music."

"I'm up for it," David announced boldly.

Emily and Jessica didn't need their arms

twisted. "Rules are made to be broken, that's my motto," Jessica declared. "How 'bout you, Liz?"

Elizabeth was gazing thoughtfully at Lina, curious about Lina's sudden, unexpected animation and about what she'd started to say: "I haven't been to Mondo in the longest *time.*" *An odd remark for a poor working-class girl from Liverpool!* "Hmm? Yeah, sure," Elizabeth told Jessica. "Count me in."

"This is going to be so much fun!" Emily exclaimed. Then her face fell. "There's only one problem."

"Mrs. Bates?" Jessica guessed.

"I'm confident that between the six of us we can come up with a scheme to fool her. No, I was thinking about . . . *her.*" Emily nodded toward the corner table.

They all turned to gaze at Portia. If she was aware of their scrutiny, she didn't show it. Daintily licking the tip of one red-nailed finger, Portia turned a page in her novel and once again raised it high.

"She'll snitch on us," Emily predicted gloomily. "She'll get us evicted from HIS."

"It's true we can't sneak out without her knowing," said Elizabeth. "So we need to get her on our side. Why not ask her to come along?"

Emily wrinkled her nose in distaste. "Hmph."

"It may be our best shot," Lina agreed reluctantly.

"*I'm* not asking her," Jessica told Elizabeth. "But if you want to set yourself up to get shot down, go ahead."

75

Elizabeth rose to her feet and strode purposefully toward Portia's table. *We're going to be roommates all month,* she reasoned. *It would be nice to be friends, too. Maybe I just didn't try hard enough last night.*

"Portia, hi," Elizabeth said.

One long beat passed, and then Portia lowered her book to nose level. The gray eyes that met Elizabeth's were expressionless. Without speaking, Portia arched her eyebrows inquiringly.

"Um, the rest of us were just— We were talking about— There's a great band playing tonight at Mondo," Elizabeth stuttered. "A friend of Gabriello's plays bass and we thought— It'll be after curfew but maybe we can sneak— Would you like to come along?" she finished in an incoherent rush.

Portia let a few more seconds tick by, seeming to enjoy watching Elizabeth squirm. "You all have a good time," she drawled, mimicking an American accent. "I personally prefer not to rub shoulders with the hoi polloi. But don't worry, I won't tattle to Mrs. Bates." In an unmistakable sign of dismissal, her eyes dropped from Elizabeth's face back to the pages of her book. "*That's* beneath me, too."

"Well, fine," Elizabeth muttered.

Whirling, she marched off, fuming silently. *See if I ever try talking to you again, Portia Albert! Who do you think you are?*

Chapter 6

At quarter past eleven that night, Jessica, Elizabeth, Emily, and Lina tiptoed down the dark staircase. David and Gabriello were waiting for them in the shadows on the second-floor landing. "So, who's going to lift Mrs. Bates's key?" whispered Gabriello.

"I am," Lina whispered back.

"How?" asked David.

"Watch this," said Lina.

With Lina leading, the six crept down to the foyer. As the others huddled in the dark dining room, Lina knocked loudly on Mrs. Bates's door across the hall. "Who is it?" Mrs. Bates called out suspiciously.

"Mrs. Bates, it's me, Lina. I have a terrible headache and I know I won't be able to sleep a wink if I don't get rid of it."

Jessica and Elizabeth peered out from the dining room, watching breathlessly. When Mrs. Bates yanked her door open, light spilled suddenly into the hallway. The twins jumped back, clutching each other and trying desperately not to giggle.

"Do you have any aspirin, Mrs. Bates?" Lina asked in a mouselike and apologetic manner.

Mrs. Bates pulled the belt of her bathrobe more snugly around her plump middle. "Come in, dear, come in," she invited impatiently. "Now, you wouldn't have a headache in the first place if you didn't squander your time tending to those ungrateful, good-for-nothing . . ."

Her voice trailed off as she shuffled across the floor, Lina trotting after her. A minute later, Lina reappeared. With her right hand, she waved an aspirin bottle at Mrs. Bates; her left arm was bent, her fist held behind her back. "Good night, Mrs. Bates. Thanks again—you're very kind."

Lina backed out of Mrs. Bates's room. The instant the door clicked shut, the others exploded out of their hiding place. "While Mrs. B. fetched the aspirin, I switched my room key for the front door key she keeps on a hook by the door." Lina displayed the purloined key triumphantly. "I'll switch them back in the morning when I return the pills. Now let's get out of here before the old hen pops out and catches us standing here!"

The well-oiled front door swung open soundlessly and the six teenagers flew out to the sidewalk. "We're free," Jessica sang.

"Which way to Mondo?" asked Elizabeth.

Gabriello pointed west. "It's walking distance,

but I say we head to the corner and hail a cab. Let's do this in style!"

They squeezed into the first taxi that came along. Elizabeth gazed out at the bright city lights blazing by, a rapt expression on her face. *We're going to dance until dawn, and Mrs. Bates will be none the wiser,* she thought, feeling daring and sophisticated. *Wait till I tell Todd and Enid about this!*

In a few minutes, the cabbie pulled up in front of a renovated warehouse marked by a neon globe proclaiming: MONDO. Elizabeth, Jessica, and the others piled out onto the sidewalk and joined the queue waiting to be admitted to the club.

Elizabeth eyed the stylish young people, suddenly feeling provincial in her plain, short knit dress. "It looks like a pretty hip crowd."

"It's *the* place in London if you want to see and be seen," Emily promised. "The people watching will be fantastic, I guarantee!"

"But we're here for the music," Gabriello reminded her as they received the nod from the bouncer and squeezed through the door.

"Speak for yourself," Emily teased, winking at Jessica.

The dark, smoky club was packed with bodies and pulsing with music. Strobe lights flashed, illuminating funky outfits, wild hairstyles, animated faces. "The dance floor is that way," Gabriello shouted, gesturing. "That's Basil's band playing right now. Let's head over!"

They pushed through the crowd, Jessica pausing occasionally to elbow Emily or Elizabeth in the ribs. "Look at that dress!" Jessica gaped at a girl in a leopard-print mini with holes cut down the front to her belly button. "Even Lila wouldn't show that much skin."

"How 'bout that one?" Emily pointed to a dress of black velvet and chiffon that looked to Elizabeth as if someone had gone at it with a pair of scissors.

"Ohmigod." Looking the other way, Jessica yanked on Emily's arm. "Em, isn't that . . . ?"

Emily clapped a hand to her mouth. "Lady Anne Binghamton. Her photo is *always* in the tabloids. She used to date Prince Malcolm!"

"Actually, she dated Malcolm's younger brother, Douglas," Lina corrected.

Emily snapped her fingers. "Right."

"There sure are some great-looking guys here," Jessica observed happily. "None as handsome as Robert Pembroke, of course, but still. Check *him* out."

Following Jessica's gaze, Emily gasped again. "I know that face," she declared. "It's . . . it's . . ." Elizabeth could see her mentally thumbing through the last issue of her favorite British celebrity magazine. "It's Percy Camden, the prime minister's son!"

"No." Once more, Lina shook her head. "I'm pretty sure that's Harry, the prime minister's *nephew*."

Emily raised her eyebrows. "Why, Lina, I had no idea you were on a first-name basis with the young London jet set!" she teased.

Lina smiled sheepishly. "What can I say, Em? Your bad habits are rubbing off—I've taken to fishing your tabloid newspapers out of the trash and reading them myself."

Within moments, Jessica and Emily were approached by two passably cute boys. As they melted into the hot whirl of bodies on the dance floor, Gabriello spotted his girlfriend, Sophie, and followed.

That left Elizabeth, Lina, and David. *Two's company, three's a crowd,* Elizabeth thought as she caught David gazing hopefully at Lina.

"Go on, you guys—take a spin," Elizabeth suggested with an encouraging smile. "I think I'll buy a soda."

"No," Lina said quickly, "you two should dance. I'm happy just listening to the music."

"So am I," David announced, clearly determined to stay by Lina's side. "I like this band. They remind me a little of a group from Liverpool. Monkeyshines—heard of 'em?"

"Um, no, I don't think so," said Lina.

"Where do you go to hear music in Liverpool?" David asked her.

Lina shifted her feet, looking poised for flight. "I don't think we're from the same part of town. We probably hang out at different pubs."

"Liverpool's not that big a city," David persisted amiably. "Try me."

"You wouldn't— Hi, Em! Hi, Jess!" Lina greeted the two returning girls with distinct relief. "Having fun?"

"Are we ever," declared Emily, lifting her auburn hair off her neck and fanning herself with one hand. "The music's outrageous. You've got to dance, all of you."

"Isn't Gabriello's friend Basil cute, Liz?" Jessica asked. "I can't wait till the band takes a break so I can meet him."

"Good luck tearing Gabriello away from Sophie long enough to get an introduction!" joked Emily. Then her gaze shifted from Gabriello and Sophie to another glamorous couple on the dance floor. "Ohmigod, *look*! It's Princess Gloria!" she squealed, pointing. "I was dancing right near her and I didn't even realize it!"

Jessica, Elizabeth, and David turned to gape. The beautiful young woman in high heels and a short, black sequined dress wore her fair hair piled loosely on top of her head; jewels glittered at her ears, throat, and wrists. "Wow," Jessica breathed.

"She's twenty-one—the queen's older daughter," said Emily. "There are pictures of her in magazines all the time—I can't believe I'm seeing her in *person*!"

It was pretty exciting, Elizabeth had to admit. Living in southern California, she and Jessica were used to spotting celebrities, but there was something special about royalty—unquestionably, Princess Gloria was more intriguing than any Hollywood movie star.

"What do you natives think about the royal family?" Elizabeth asked David and Lina. "Lina, had you ever— Are you all right?"

82

Lina's face was ghostly pale; she looked as if all the blood had been suddenly drained from her body. Elizabeth put a hand on her friend's arm and repeated the question. "Lina, are you OK?"

"No." Lina shook her head. "I don't feel well—I don't feel well at all. I'd better go home. Now!"

Abruptly, Lina spun on her heel and darted toward the exit. "I'll go with her," Elizabeth offered. "It's late. Maybe we should all go."

"But I'm not ready to leave yet!" Jessica wailed. "We just got here—I want to dance. I want to meet the guys in the band!"

"Tell you what—we'll leave the front-door key under the flowerpot," Elizabeth proposed. "Just don't stay out *too* late. We managed to sneak out undetected, but Mrs. Bates gets up at the crack of dawn. You wouldn't want her to catch you sneaking back *in*!"

Elizabeth caught up to Lina on the sidewalk just outside Mondo. "Lina, wait!"

A chill fog had crept into the city while they were inside; Lina's woolly cardigan was buttoned up to her neck. Elizabeth was relieved to see some color in her cheeks, however. "You look better," she said.

Lina nodded. "I *feel* better. For a minute in there, I thought I was going to faint. I guess I just needed some fresh air."

"You should probably go straight to bed." Fumbling in her pocketbook, Elizabeth was only able to come up with some small change. "Shoot. I don't have enough money for a cab."

Lina pulled the empty pockets of her cardigan inside out. "Me, either. But it's probably just a fifteen-minute walk back to HIS. The exercise will do me good."

They headed east into the fog. Two blocks from Mondo, they turned right onto Spencer Street. "This is a nice residential neighborhood," said Lina. "And it should connect straight through to Winchester."

The fog, curling thickly around trees and houses, dimmed the yellow globes of the street lamps. Cold, white fingers of mist brushed the girls' faces and sprinkled their hair with dew; they walked quickly and close together.

"I'm sorry to tear you away from all the fun," Lina apologized. "You're very sweet to look after me."

"It works out just fine," Elizabeth assured her. "This way, I'll be well rested for another day at the *Journal*." Her lips curved in a smile. "Anyhow, I'm sure there'll be other midnight escapades!"

"It's a fun bunch at HIS, isn't it?" Lina agreed.

"I like everyone a lot." Elizabeth thought of Portia Albert. "Well, *almost* everyone." She glanced at Lina out of the corner of her eye. "David is really nice, isn't he? The two of you must have a lot to talk about, being from the same hometown and all. And he's awfully cute."

A telltale blush stained Lina's fair cheeks. "Umm," she murmured. "He *is* that."

"You know, I think he likes you," Elizabeth ventured.

Lina hunched her slender shoulders, tucking her chin into the neck of her sweater. "He's a pleasant fellow. So sweet and serious . . . so different from other boys I've known. But I'm *not* looking for a boyfriend this summer," she added emphatically.

Something about Lina's tone discouraged further discussion. *What* are *you looking for?* Elizabeth wondered, deciding that underneath her plain surface, Lina Smith was really a very complicated girl.

They crossed a couple of side streets and then the road ended in a T. "Spencer dead-ends here," Lina observed. "We can go left or right but not straight."

Elizabeth peered through the fog at the cross streets. "Rochester. Does that ring a bell?"

"'Fraid not." Lina bit her lip. "But I think HIS is over . . . there." She waved a hand vaguely. "I say we turn left."

Elizabeth glanced back over her shoulder. The mist had closed in behind them, obliterating the path they'd just taken. The swirling white made her dizzy and disoriented. *We're lost—lost in the English fog,* Elizabeth thought, her heart contracting. *Just like the boys in the werewolf movie . . .* "Left is fine with me. I've lost all sense of direction, anyway."

They proceeded on, their steps tentative. The dense blanket of fog muffled all sound; the street was eerily silent, and the girls fell silent, too.

Suddenly, the night was shattered by a high-pitched shriek. Elizabeth's heart leapt into her throat; with a cry of fear, she grabbed Lina's arm.

A black cat sprang out of the mist, darting across the sidewalk in front of them. The two girls collapsed against each other, laughing with relief. "A cat. It was just a cat," Lina gasped.

Elizabeth took a deep breath to slow the pounding of her heart. "Look at us, scared to death by a little fog."

"It's too silly. C'mon." Lina hooked her arm through Elizabeth's. "Let's step lively, or we'll never get home!"

They lengthened their strides and Lina began whistling softly. Elizabeth knew her companion was still just as edgy as she was, though; the muscles in Lina's arm were tense, and her eyes darted continually from side to side.

And then Lina stopped dead in her tracks and screamed—a scream of pure terror that raked Elizabeth's nerves with teeth of ice. "Look," Lina choked, pointing with a trembling finger.

Something lay on the edge of the sidewalk—a tiny, crumpled, furry body. "It's a dog," Elizabeth whispered. "A dead dog." Then she saw the distinctive jeweled collar . . . and something else that made her blood run cold.

"Poo-Poo," she murmered. It was Lady Wimpole's missing Yorkshire terrier . . . dead, with his throat ripped out.

Elizabeth closed her eyes, swallowing hard.

Lina was crying softly. "Poor little thing. That horrible gash—it almost looks as if he were attacked by a wild animal. But how could that happen here in London?"

Elizabeth shuddered. *Attacked by a wild animal* . . .

Just then, a beam of light shone down on the body of the hapless dog. Glancing up fearfully, Elizabeth saw the moon glinting through a ragged break in the clouds. It was pale yellow . . . and nearly full.

Suddenly, the old bag lady's words of warning echoed in her head. *Beware the full moon. . . .*

"So, then what did you do?" asked Jessica in a horrified whisper.

After much tossing and turning, Lina had finally fallen asleep, but Elizabeth continued to lie awake, restless and troubled by the light of the moon coming through her window . . . and by the thought of Poo-Poo's dreadful end.

She was thankful when Jessica tiptoed in and sat on the edge of her bunk to tell her about all the boys she'd danced with at Mondo. It was a relief to tell someone about Poo-Poo.

"I had my camera and mini-corder in my bag," Elizabeth whispered back, "so I did what Lucy did at Dr. Neville's—I took some pictures and recorded a description. Meanwhile, Lina ran to the nearest telephone booth—thank goodness they're painted red, or she never would have found one in the fog!"

"What did the police say?"

"They weren't terribly interested. They took the

address from Lina and said they'd send an animal-control car over in the morning to pick up the body and take it to Lady Wimpole's." Elizabeth shivered. "They didn't seem to understand that he hadn't just been hit by a car, that . . . something else . . . had happened to him."

"Poor Poo-Poo. Poor Lady Wimpole!"

"She's going to be heartbroken." Elizabeth's throat tightened with tears. "It was horrible, Jess," she whispered.

"I'm telling you, Liz, it's werewolf season," Jessica said lightly. "Just like in the movie we watched at Lila's. Looks like Poo-Poo tried to make friends with the wrong kind of dog!"

Elizabeth tried to laugh, but it came out sounding more like a sob.

Jessica squeezed her sister's arm. "Don't take it so hard," she advised gently. "It's too bad about Poo-Poo, but there's nothing anyone can do for him now."

Elizabeth nodded without speaking.

Rising, Jessica slipped off her dress and pulled on an oversized sleep T-shirt. The bunk squeaked as she clambered on top. Almost instantly, Elizabeth heard a muffled snore from above.

As Jessica said, there's no point fretting, Elizabeth told herself. *No one can help Poo-Poo now. Just go to sleep. Stop worrying . . .*

But she couldn't stop worrying; she couldn't stop puzzling over the mysteries that suddenly seemed to haunt her. Dr. Neville's murder and its downplayed coverage in the *Journal,* and now Poo-Poo . . .

One thing was for certain, Elizabeth thought. Movies were one thing, and real life was another. Jessica wouldn't have laughed if she'd been there in the fog on Spencer Street, if she'd seen the dog's twisted, mutilated corpse with her own eyes. Who—or what—had done that to him?

Chapter 7

"I suppose we can't sneak out every night," Gabriello murmured to Jessica as they stood in the HIS foyer after breakfast on Tuesday, "because I'm going to fall asleep in class. But it really was a blast."

Jessica nodded, rubbing her eyes. "I'd better get an easy assignment at the *Journal* today—something that doesn't involve much walking or talking." She yawned widely. "Maybe a story about the important health benefits of taking an afternoon nap!" The yawn was contagious; Elizabeth, Emily, Lina, and David all followed suit.

As the six shuffled with heavy footsteps to the front door, they were overtaken by Rene, looking crisp and elegant in a double-breasted, navy-blue summer suit. Stopping by Elizabeth's side, he put a hand on her arm. "I'm late already, or I'd offer to escort you to work," he said, his eyes bright. "My only consolation is our dinner date this evening—I look forward so much to finally having a chance to talk with you."

Elizabeth gave him a sleepy smile. "Me, too, Rene."

He waved to the others. "Have a great day, everyone!"

As Rene strode off briskly, Emily put her hands on her hips and shook her head. "Astonishing, simply astonishing," she declared. "Lord Robert Pembroke, Rene Glize . . . you Wakefields have managed to snag all the gorgeous guys already. American girls have all the luck!"

"I wonder what Lucy will give us today?" Jessica said to Elizabeth as they waved to Tony Frank on their way to the crime editor's desk.

"I want to tell her about Poo-Poo," said Elizabeth. "Maybe she'll let us do a follow-up with Lady Wimpole."

When they didn't find Lucy at her desk, the twins wandered back toward Tony's cubicle. As they passed a glass-windowed conference room, Jessica halted, gripping her sister's arm. "There she is, with Reeves."

As if someone had yanked it shut in a hurry, the curtain over the conference-room window wasn't closed all the way. An inch or two of window remained uncovered—just enough for Jessica and Elizabeth to peek through.

"This is some heavy-duty meeting," Elizabeth whispered. "Lucy looks really mad!"

They couldn't hear what Lucy was saying, but her gestures and expression spoke volumes. Tossing her hair, she stalked up and down, her eyes flashing angrily. Words spilled from her lips in a furious torrent.

Strangely enough, in the face of this display, Henry Reeves appeared calm and undisturbed. Hands folded, he sat at the conference table quietly watching Lucy pace.

"How can he be so mellow when she's so upset?" Jessica wondered.

"Maybe that's *why* she's so upset," Elizabeth guessed. "Whatever it is she's saying, he's not listening."

Lucy raised her voice, her words reaching the twins through the conference room's thick, nearly soundproof window. "I quit!" Lucy shouted, flinging her arms into the air.

Jessica and Elizabeth glanced at each other, shocked. Reeves didn't so much as blink an eye. Nor did he try to prevent Lucy from storming from the room—his lips remained pressed together in a stern, thin line.

The conference room door banged open and Lucy burst out, her hazel eyes shooting sparks. The twins flattened themselves against the wall, hoping it wasn't too obvious that they'd been spying. It didn't matter; Lucy didn't see them. With the momentum of a freight train, she careened off down the hallway, her tawny hair bouncing and her high heels clattering.

Jessica and Elizabeth hurried after her, not wanting to miss any of the action. As Lucy swept past Tony's cubicle, he called after her. "Friday, what's wrong?"

"I'm quitting, Frank," she shot back, not slowing her pace. "And don't try to talk me out of it!"

Leaping to his feet, Tony joined Jessica and Elizabeth in chasing Lucy back to her desk. Without a moment's hesitation, Lucy began sweeping her personal belongings into a roomy, battered leather attaché.

"Now, Friday, take a deep breath," Tony urged in a soothing tone. He placed a hand on her arm. "Let's talk this through. What set you off this time?"

Lucy shook off his hand impatiently. Yanking the top drawer right out of her desk, she upended it into the attaché. "You know darned well what set me off, Frank. One of the most shocking and mysterious murders in years, and Reeves hides the story at the back of the paper!"

"It was a big news day, what with the princess still missing," Tony reasoned. "Perhaps Reeves thought the murder story didn't rate—"

"And he didn't just edit my piece—he didn't just trim it," Lucy interrupted, pausing in her cleanup to slam a fist on the desk. "He butchered it! He left out all the pertinent details such as—"

Tony cleared his throat loudly, shooting a pointed glance at the twins, and Lucy caught herself. *Such as Dr. Neville's gruesomely ravaged throat*, Elizabeth thought, gulping.

"He made it sound as if Neville could have died of natural causes. It's a cover-up, plain and simple,

94

and I've had enough. I won't work for a dishonest newspaper."

"Now, Friday." Tony lifted a hand to gently push back a strand of Lucy's tousled hair. "Let's not be so hot and hasty. You've worked hard to build a career—don't throw it away on a whim. Reeves revised your story, granted, but that doesn't necessarily indicate—"

"Don't defend him, Frank," Lucy warned. "You know as well as I do that Reeves is in a sweat about the competition from the *Post*. This isn't the first time he's . . ."

Jessica and Elizabeth strained to hear what came next, but Lucy had lowered her voice. She and Tony moved off slightly, continuing their conversation out of earshot.

"A cover-up at the *London Journal*!" Jessica whispered excitedly.

"And Henry Reeves himself is behind it!" Elizabeth whispered back.

"So, while Liz is writing up the dead dog story, what should *I* do?" Jessica asked Tony.

Lucy had exited the office like a tornado, leaving a ransacked desk and a trail of whispers in her wake. A mere twenty-four hours after first arriving at the *London Journal*, the twins were under Tony Frank's wing once more.

"Well, let's see. I may have an upper-crust tea party for you," he kidded.

"I know I was kind of scornful about writing for the society page yesterday," Jessica said contritely, hitching herself up on the edge of Tony's desk. "But as it turns out, I think I'll be very well-suited to it. You see, I now have an *in* with the aristocracy. I'm *dating* the younger Lord Robert Pembroke."

Tony looked suitably impressed. "That was fast. Swept him off his feet, eh?"

"He's putty in my hands."

Tony dropped into his desk chair. "Putty, eh? Somehow, I never thought of young Pembroke as being made of a soft, malleable substance," he reflected. "I would have said he was more the unpredictable volcanic type."

"Really?" Jessica said with interest. "Do you know him?"

"He's the *Journal* owner's only son and heir-apparent, that's all," Tony said carelessly. "Though he doesn't toe the line as much as Lord P. Senior would like."

"How do you mean?"

"He's sowed some wild oats and rumor has it old Bob worries that he won't ever settle down to being a proper lord of the manor and newspaper owner. I say give the boy a chance—blood will tell."

. Wild oats . . . blood will tell. Jessica was more intrigued by Lord Pembroke Junior than ever. She felt a pleasant shiver of anticipation. *And I'm having dinner with him tonight!*

"Don't get me wrong—I've always liked the chap." Tony winked at Jessica. "And I'd say he's shaping up already, casting his eye on one of my star interns. Speaking of which, before I send you

96

off on assignment, let's just check Lucy's desk in case she left anything behind for you."

Lucy's desk was a mess of scrap paper: half-written stories and notes relating to matters she'd deemed unimportant. "But she took her file on the Dr. Neville murder," Tony murmured to himself. "Hmm . . ."

Next to the telephone was a small notepad. As Tony read the top sheet, his lips twitched with amusement. "Lucy didn't forget you, see? 'Liz and Jessica, Scotland Yard, shoplifting chauffeur case.' Here's the address. You're all set."

"Oh, no," groaned Jessica. "Don't tell me."

"I'm afraid so." Tony's grin widened. "It's a Sergeant Bumpo case!"

"Thank you for talking to me, Lady Wimpole," said Elizabeth. "I know how hard this must be for you."

Replacing the phone, Elizabeth resumed typing, her brow furrowed. "The Wimpole family does not know who might have had a motive to harm them or their pet," she murmured as her fingers flew over the keyboard. "Nor has it been determined whether the terrier ran away or was abducted. His body was found more than three miles from Knightsbridge on Spencer Street. . . ."

Just typing the words "Spencer Street" gave Elizabeth goose bumps. She could almost feel the clammy fog closing around her; she could almost hear Lina's bloodcurdling scream. . . .

A hand touched Elizabeth's shoulder, and she

nearly jumped out of her skin. "Oh, Luke, it's you!" she squeaked.

"I did it again," he said ruefully. "I'm always scaring you!"

"I was already scared," Elizabeth confessed, "just reliving last night."

Quickly, she told him about sneaking out after curfew, and walking home from Mondo in the fog with Lina. "I recognized the little dog right away, from the photos Lady Wimpole showed us. And he wore a little leather collar with gemstones. . . ." Elizabeth crossed her arms, hugging herself. "His throat was torn open, just like—" She stopped herself, remembering that Luke didn't know the true details of Dr. Neville's death. "It was awful."

Luke narrowed his eyes. "What do you mean, his throat was torn open? You mean, with a knife?"

"No, it wasn't a clean cut. The wound was . . ." She shuddered. "Jagged."

"Jagged, as if perhaps . . ." A worried frown creased Luke's forehead; his eyes clouded.

"Luke, what is it?" Elizabeth asked. "What are you thinking?"

Luke blinked. "Nothing," he said, though he still appeared troubled. "Nothing."

An instant later, his expression cleared and he smiled. "Tell you what. Finish typing your story and then ask Tony if he'll give you the afternoon off. I'll take you sight-seeing."

Fortunately, Tony was amenable to the idea. "Get to know the city," he urged Elizabeth. "It will help make you a better reporter."

Luke and Elizabeth grabbed their sweaters and headed for the door. "Now, forget about last night," Luke ordered Elizabeth. "London is a warm and delightful city by daylight, I promise!"

Warm and delightful . . . I don't know about that, Elizabeth thought as she and Luke wandered through the vast, shadowy, echoing spaces of Westminster Abbey.

The abbey was certainly awe-inspiringly beautiful, and rich with history. "I can't believe how many famous people are buried in here!" Elizabeth whispered to Luke as they paused to read the memorial stones in the poets' corner. "Kings and queens, writers and statesmen . . . I've never seen anything like it."

"Think of all the ceremonies that have taken place here over the centuries," he murmured back. "Royal weddings, and christenings, and funeral processions. The stained-glass windows, the vaulting arches, the very stones under our feet have silently witnessed it all for hundreds and hundreds of years."

Despite her fuzzy cardigan sweater, Elizabeth felt chilled to the bones. "I'm ready for some sunshine," she told Luke. "What's the next stop on our tour?"

"The Tower of London," Luke answered, taking her arm. "I'll tell you about it on the way over."

The day was warm and clear, so they walked to the tower, pausing on a bridge spanning the Thames River to savor the view from a distance.

"Kings and queens, starting with William the Conqueror in the eleventh century, used the tower buildings as a prison," Luke explained. "Mary, Queen of Scots, was beheaded there in 1587 for conspiring to seize the English throne from the rightful queen, your namesake, Elizabeth I."

Arriving at the tower, they purchased tickets and joined a guided tour. "I'm sure the tour guide will tell the story of the little princes," Luke said to Elizabeth in a low voice as they crossed a stone courtyard. Huge black ravens perched on a wall, cawing mournfully. "It's featured in Shakespeare's historical play about Richard the Third. Do you know it?"

Elizabeth shook her head. "Who were the little princes?"

"The sons of Richard's older brother, King Edward the Fourth. The tragedy unfolded during the Wars of the Roses, in the fifteenth century. Upon Edward's death, Richard seized power, declaring himself the young princes' protector." Luke laughed mirthlessly. "Some protector. He had the little boys imprisoned here . . . and then he ordered them murdered."

Elizabeth gasped. "How horrible!"

"Or so the story goes," Luke concluded in a lighter tone. "Some modern-day historians claim that Richard wasn't quite as villainous as Shakespeare made him out. They never did find the bodies of the little boys. . . ."

As they entered a dimly lit passageway, Elizabeth glanced fearfully over her shoulder. Shadows danced on the dank stone walls; she could almost imagine they were the ghosts of the murdered princes. "What a gruesome place," she said, shuddering. "It must have been so awful to be imprisoned here, knowing you might moulder and die in one of these dark cells, never again seeing the light of day."

"Or perhaps you'd see the light of day one last time, as they led you in chains to that courtyard where the ravens were—in order to behead you."

"I can't imagine living in such a brutal time," Elizabeth reflected.

"It's fascinating, though, isn't it?" said Luke. "Throughout history, the things people have done to their own flesh and blood out of greed, ambition, jealousy, fear."

"Fascinating," Elizabeth agreed, "but also frightening!"

After admiring the crown jewels, housed in the tower for safekeeping, Elizabeth and Luke hurried back outside. "There's one more place I'd like to show you," said Luke.

Elizabeth laughed. "As long as it doesn't have any graves or dungeons. I've had my share of old bones for the day, thank you very much!"

Luke grinned. "No old bones, I promise. It's history, in a way, but just for fun."

A few minutes later, they stood on the sidewalk in front of the wax museum. As Luke paid for two tickets, Elizabeth smiled. "You tricked me," she teased. "There are bound to be lots of murderous scenes depicted in here."

"But they're just wax dummies. It's not real blood!"

The wax museum proved highly entertaining. Elizabeth was captivated by the wax models of British royalty, from the unfortunate wives of Henry VIII to the present-day queen and her family. "The costumes are wonderful," she exclaimed, curtsying to the wax queen. "That's just the sort of funny little hat she always wears!"

"They make new models of the royal family's younger members every year or so," Luke told her, "and I believe the family donates the clothes so the dioramas will be authentic."

Elizabeth gazed thoughtfully at the model of Princess Eliana, the queen's youngest daughter, who was still missing. "I wonder where she is?" she mused.

They moved on, past famous characters from fiction, film, and folklore, as well as history. As they moved back in time, the path grew dimmer; flickering candles replaced the electric lighting, creating an aura of mystery and suspense. Elizabeth's scalp prickled. *What will be around the next bend in the hall?* she wondered.

When she saw the next exhibit, she clutched Luke's arm. "A werewolf!" she cried.

The figures of the diorama illustrated the stages of the werewolf's terrifying transformation, from ordinary man to a hairy, crouching, red-eyed creature with blood dripping from its fangs. *It's so lifelike,* Elizabeth thought. *It looks like it might spring right out at us.*

She buried her face against Luke's woolly sweater. "Let's get out of here," she whispered.

"In a minute," Luke murmured, wrapping a strong arm around her shoulders. "It's just wax, remember, Liz? Look up. It won't hurt you."

Reluctantly, Elizabeth turned back to the exhibit, but she remained pressed close to Luke's side. "The werewolf is one of the most fascinating creatures in all folklore," said Luke. "The superstition dates back to medieval times. The transformation from man to wolf is performed at will in some cases; in others, it's involuntary, triggered by passion or the phases of the moon. The full moon, of course, is when the werewolf comes into possession of his greatest powers—his greatest strength and ferocity. It's when he kills."

Elizabeth clenched her teeth to keep them from chattering. "You know an awful lot about this." She forced a nervous laugh. "I guess you've seen more than one werewolf movie!"

"It's an interest of mine," Luke admitted. "I picked it up from my mother—she was intrigued by the legends. She collected books and artifacts relating to the subject." Luke pulled a wolf-fang keychain from his pocket and held it up for Elizabeth to see. "This belonged to her. Do you think it's a strange hobby, Elizabeth?"

She shrugged. "I . . . I guess not."

"I'd understand if you thought it odd," he assured her. "I'm sure *your* mother doesn't believe in werewolves! But I've never been able to forget something my mother once said to me. She believed that to acknowledge the reality of the werewolf is merely to acknowledge our own dual nature. Mankind is composed of both heaven and hell; we are bad as well as good. We *all* have an animal side, Elizabeth."

Elizabeth nodded, her eyes on Luke's face. He continued talking softly. "Like vampires, werewolves are immortal and indestructible. They often pass their curse on to their unfortunate victims, who become un-dead."

"Isn't there any way to stop them?" wondered Elizabeth.

"The curse can only be lifted if the werewolf's bloodline is severed—if the werewolf himself is destroyed, by fire or by a weapon made of pure silver, such as a silver bullet."

Luke spoke matter-of-factly, as if there were no doubt in his mind that werewolves were real. Elizabeth knew she should be skeptical—she remembered scoffing at Jessica. *An American Werewolf in London* was only a movie. . . . But after an afternoon spent immersed in the shadowy side of England's past, she didn't *feel* skeptical. She was entranced by Luke's words; they entered her mind in a strange way, taking root. *History is full of murderous monsters, human and nonhuman,* she thought, still staring, mesmerized, at the figure of the werewolf. *Who am I to say werewolves don't exist?*

Chapter 8

When Elizabeth and Luke emerged from the wax museum, the sun had dropped behind the buildings, sinking the city streets in shadow. A cool, slightly damp breeze fingered Elizabeth's hair. *It's going to be another foggy night,* she guessed. *A good night to get home early . . . and stay home!*

"Is it really that late?" Luke asked as the bells of a nearby church chimed the hour. "We didn't have any tea—you must be ravenous."

"I wouldn't mind a bite to eat," Elizabeth admitted.

"Then do me the honor of dining with me," Luke said gallantly. "There's a wonderful old pub a few streets from here—a bit fancier than the Slaughtered Lamb. They have a fireplace big enough to roast an ox—it'll warm you up in no time."

The invitation was enough to make Elizabeth

feel warm inside. The wax museum had given her the creeps, but she couldn't deny she'd enjoyed an excuse to be close to Luke. She was happy to extend their excursion for an hour or two longer. "Sounds divine," she said with a smile. "But what about your father? Isn't he expecting you for dinner?"

Luke shook his head. "I tend to come and go as I please. He won't wait for me—we rarely have a meal together."

Tactfully, Elizabeth let the subject drop. Luke's tone verged on gruff; it didn't encourage further inquiry. *Poor guy,* she thought, her heart swelling with pity. *To be motherless, and for all purposes fatherless, too!*

The Gloucester Arms was bustling and bright. Within minutes, Luke and Elizabeth were tucked away at a cozy corner table, big plates of hearty stew and crusty homemade bread in front of them. Slipping out of her cardigan, Elizabeth dug into her food, suddenly starving.

"I feel like I haven't eaten in days," she said, tearing off another piece of the warm bread. "I guess all the excitement at the *Journal* is giving me an appetite."

"You mean Lady Wimpole's dog?"

Elizabeth gazed somberly at Luke. He looked back with clear, honest eyes. *I might as well tell him,* she decided. *Maybe he can help me make sense of it all.* "The dog is only part of it. You heard that Lucy Friday quit, didn't you?"

"Sure. Everyone at work was talking about it. She had a falling-out with old man Reeves."

106

"That's an understatement." Elizabeth leaned forward, lowering her voice. "Lucy accused Reeves of covering up the murder of Dr. Neville. He suppressed her story of what really happened—that's why she quit."

Luke's eyes widened. "What really happened? You mean, they know more than they printed?"

Elizabeth nodded. "*Lots* more. And Jessica and I know it, too, because we were there . . . at Dr. Neville's house. We looked in the window and saw . . . and saw . . ." Suddenly, the memory seemed too terrible. She couldn't go on.

"What?" Luke prompted gently. "What did you see?"

"Doctor Neville lying on the floor, dead. Lucy was there, and two men—Lord Robert Pembroke Senior, who owns the *Journal*, and Andrew Thatcher, the chief of the London police."

Firelight flickered on Luke's face; Elizabeth saw his jaw tighten. "What else? How did Neville die?"

"There was blood everywhere." Elizabeth pressed her hands to her eyes as if she could wipe out the vision. "The body was facedown, but Lucy must have seen . . . the other side. She said into her tape recorder that—that the doctor looked as if he'd been attacked by a wild animal."

"Meaning . . . ?"

"His throat was torn out," Elizabeth whispered. "Just like Poo-Poo's."

The color drained from Luke's face. "I didn't want to believe it," he said, his voice hoarse. "I didn't say anything when you told me about the dog, but this—this confirms my worst fears."

"Your fears about what?" asked Elizabeth, her heart thumping wildly.

"The deaths—Dr. Neville's and the little Yorkie's. I think they're connected somehow." Luke's eyes were wide and frightened. "And it sounds like the work of a . . ."

Elizabeth braced herself for his next words. A draft of clammy air brushed her bare arms; her whole body trembled.

" . . . a werewolf!"

"It can't be," Elizabeth breathed.

"Have you seen wolves at the zoo being fed? Have you seen them tear into the meat with their fangs? The wounds you've described weren't made by any ordinary weapon. And a dog will bark at a werewolf. Poo-Poo may have . . . antagonized . . ."

Elizabeth pictured the encounter and shivered again. The theory was incredibly farfetched, but Luke managed to be very convincing. "So, why the cover-up?" She pushed back her plate, her appetite gone. "Do you think Lord Pembroke knows something about it?"

"Pembroke." Luke spat out the name, startling Elizabeth with his vehemence. "He was viewing the the body—he must know something," he declared. "And he owns the *Journal*. It's common knowledge that he has immense influence over Reeves and editorial decisions. The chief of police was there, too, you say? Yes." Luke nodded, his expression grim. "Pembroke's involved, I'm sure of it. For some reason, he's making both Reeves and the police department cover up the murder of Dr. Neville!"

"I keep thinking I must be dreaming," Jessica said to Emily on Tuesday evening. Taking one of her sister's silk blouses from the closet, she held it up to herself in front of the mirror. "I mean, I never have a problem meeting guys, and I've dated some rich ones. But let's face it, nobody in California has a *title*. There aren't any lords and ladies in Sweet Valley!"

"In Sydney, either," said Emily. "Robert sounds like he stepped straight out of a fairy tale. What a story to tell your friends back home!"

"They'll die," Jessica predicted with satisfaction. "They'll just die."

She faced Emily, displaying the blouse. Emily wrinkled her freckled nose thoughtfully, then shook her head. "It's pretty, but a bit too . . . *red*."

"Too flashy, huh?" Jessica ruffled through the closet some more. "You're right. Robert's used to dating very high-class girls. I don't want to look like a cocktail waitress. Nothing too bare, nothing too bright. . . . How 'bout this?"

She held out Elizabeth's navy and white sailor dress for Emily's inspection. Once more, Emily shook her head. "Too schoolgirlish."

"Right again," Jessica agreed. "He probably thinks I'm at least eighteen, and I don't want to disillusion him!"

"Too bad Portia's such a nasty piece of work," Emily commented. "She has the most stunning wardrobe."

Jessica turned to Portia's side of the closet and sighed. "What I wouldn't give to borrow this," she said, fingering an elegant silk chemise. "With that raw silk jacket of hers over it . . ."

"And her *accessories*. Scarves, belts, shoes, hair thingimabobs—every inch of her is always perfect, from her fingernail polish to her panty hose."

Rifling in the back of the closet, Jessica came across a hanging garment bag. She unzipped it, gasping with surprised pleasure. "Now, how about this!" She showed Emily the emerald-green taffeta party dress. "It's too dressy for a dinner date, but Robert's bound to invite me to a more formal event one of these days—a function at Buckingham Palace, maybe! I'll just have to butter Portia up. I don't care what a witch she is—I have to borrow this dress."

Emily studied the dress with interest. "That can't be Portia's, though. Look how short it is in the waist—it wouldn't even fit you, and Portia's inches taller yet."

"Well, it's not mine and it's not Liz's," said Jessica. "So it must be . . ."

Emily's eyebrows shot up. Jessica's mouth dropped open. "Lina's?" said Emily, puzzled. "But where would she get the money for a dress like that?"

"Maybe someone donated it to the homeless shelter," Jessica guessed, stroking the lush fabric of the dress.

"Or maybe she . . ." Emily bit her lip, not finishing the sentence.

She didn't need to. *Maybe she stole it,* Jessica thought. *Oh, the poor, poor deprived thing, to do something so desperate!*

Just then there was a sharp rap on the door. "Put the dress away, quick!" Emily hissed. "It's Mrs. Bates—we don't want to get Lina in trouble!"

Jessica shoved the dress back in the garment bag and slammed the closet door, then threw herself into the easy chair opposite Emily's. "Come in!" she called.

Mrs. Bates stepped into the room, her expression disapproving, as usual.

"What ho, Mrs. Bates!" Emily caroled with irreverent cheeriness.

Jessica stifled a giggle. Mrs. Bates pursed her lips. "I heard that you have a *date* this evening, Jessica." She made "date" sound like a dirty word. "I hope you and your young man will not forget that we have a *curfew* here at Housing for International Students."

"Thanks for the reminder," Jessica said with a falsely sweet smile. "I'll be sure to tell my young man . . . Lord Robert Pembroke."

"*The* Lord Robert Pembroke?" Mrs. Bates croaked.

"None other," Jessica drawled. "Robert *Junior*, of course—Lord P. Senior would be much too old for me. Why, he's probably as old as you!"

The insult slipped right by Mrs. Bates, who appeared to be experiencing heart palpitations. She patted her ample bosom, and then raised her pince-nez to her nose to peer at Jessica with new

111

interest. "Why, my dear, a date with Lord Pembroke!" Mrs. Bates fluttered over to Jessica and gave her arm a motherly pat. "How splendid—how *delightful*. Well, under *these* circumstances, of course, an exception *could* be made . . . if you should be the teensy, weensiest bit late . . . I'll wait up for you, just in case. The door won't be locked against you, not while you're accompanied by Lord Robert Pembroke. . . ."

Still babbling like a brook, Mrs. Bates scurried out. The moment the door shut behind her, Jessica and Emily burst out laughing. "What a sly way to exploit the old biddy's weakness for the upper class!" Emily exclaimed. "You've got her eating out of the palm of your hand. Congratulations."

Jessica grinned. "Just chalk up another victory for the Americans!"

"Thank you for a wonderful day, Elizabeth."

Luke had ridden back with her on the tube and now they stood on the sidewalk in front of HIS. Dusk had fallen. The leafy branches of a tree blocked the light of a nearby street lamp, making it difficult for Elizabeth to read Luke's expression.

He was very close; she could feel the warmth from his body. Elizabeth's heart skipped a beat. The day's startling revelations had flung them into an unexpected intimacy; she knew she would never forget his face in the firelight at the Gloucester Arms, or the feel of his arm warm and strong around her at the wax museum.

I want him to kiss me, Elizabeth realized suddenly, glad that the shadows hid her blush. "Thanks for going out of your way to bring me home," she said. "I'll see you at work tomorrow."

"Good night." Bending his head, Luke grazed her cheek with his lips. An electric current shot through Elizabeth, warming her entire body. Then he turned and disappeared into the night mist. Elizabeth watched him go, one hand held to her burning cheek. Though the kiss had been as light and soft as the brush of a butterfly's wing, perfectly chaste and proper, it held the unmistakable promise of a real kiss in the not-too-distant future. . . .

Her head spinning, from the kiss and from all the events of the day, Elizabeth walked slowly up the path to the dorm. The front door of HIS was open, and a tall figure stood there, as if waiting for her. Elizabeth focused on the boy, and then clapped a hand to her mouth, horrified at her thoughtlessness.

"Oh, Rene!" she gasped, her face turning as red as a London phone booth. "I completely forgot about our plans. I'm so sorry! But we were sight-seeing, and I lost track of time, and . . ."

She smiled apologetically, but Rene's expression remained stiff and cool. *Did he see Luke kiss me?* she wondered, wishing she could think of a way to diffuse the awkwardness of the moment. "I'm sorry," she repeated. "Let's make a rain date. How 'bout tomorrow night?"

"I'm busy," Rene said curtly. "This was my only free evening all week."

"Oh." Elizabeth bit her lip. "Well . . ."

"I have some paperwork to do," Rene muttered. "See you around, Elizabeth."

Turning on his heel, he stalked off. With a sigh, Elizabeth trudged up the rest of the steps and into the foyer of HIS. *I guess I really let him down,* she thought with regret. *Or maybe I just hurt his pride,* she mused, heading down the hall toward the library, where she intended to curl up with a book. *Either way, he overreacted. It was a simple mistake, and it's not like he's my boyfriend. He doesn't have any claim on me.*

There was an alcove outside the library containing a chair, a small table, and a telephone. As Elizabeth approached, she heard a girl speaking. "No, Daddy, I haven't landed a part yet, but I'm going to keep on trying. . . ."

It was Portia. Elizabeth resisted the temptation to slow down as she passed by, not wanting Portia to suspect her of eavesdropping. But the fragment of conversation was tantalizing. *What about her role in* A Common Man? Elizabeth wondered. Portia had to be lying to somebody: either to her father, or to everybody in the dorm. Which was it, and why?

Elizabeth's brain was too tired to grapple with another mystery. She didn't have the mental energy to think about Portia, or about Rene, for that matter.

In the library, she crossed to a wall lined with old books and ran her eye along the titles. She chose a slim, leather-bound volume—*The Strange Case of Dr. Jekyll and Mr. Hyde* by Robert Louis

Stevenson—and then settled into an overstuffed chair by one of the tall, brocade-curtained windows. Opening the book, she skimmed a line or two but soon her gaze strayed to the reflections in the window and her thoughts turned back to the chilling mysteries of London, past and present . . . to werewolves . . . and to Luke.

"I think that was the most elegant meal I've ever eaten," Jessica confessed as Robert Pembroke helped her into the backseat of a long black limousine.

"This is my favorite restaurant in London," said Robert. Climbing in next to Jessica, he grinned up at the chauffeur. "Clifford can tell you, we stop off here at least once a week."

"We certainly do, sir," Clifford confirmed solemnly before closing the door and walking around to the driver's seat.

Jessica leaned back against the butter-soft leather upholstery. *Imagine having your very own family chauffeur to drive you around to a different fancy restaurant whenever you wanted. Every night would be like prom night,* she thought. *I think I could get used to it!*

"Where to now, sir?" Clifford inquired politely.

"Hmm . . . let's see." Robert pondered the options, tapping his jaw with his forefinger. "Fashion is so ephemeral—last week's hip spot will be dead as a doornail this week. You'll have to be my lucky charm, Jessica. I say we try Club U.S.A. on Thames Street."

When the limousine rolled to a stop in front of

Club U.S.A., Robert and Jessica waited for Clifford to walk around and open the door. Stepping out onto the sidewalk under bright neon lights, Jessica felt like a movie star arriving at a Hollywood premiere. Dozens of people clustered around the entrance, waiting to be admitted to the club. When the bouncer spotted Lord Pembroke, he waved them right in. "It pays to be a Pembroke," Robert whispered jokingly in Jessica's ear. "Stick with me, kid, and we'll go places."

Stick with you . . . don't worry, I'm planning to! Jessica thought.

The packed club's clientele was, if anything, even more glamorous than at Mondo the previous night. Immediately, Jessica spotted Princess Gloria, this time wearing a peacock-blue strapless dress. "I saw her at Mondo last night," Jessica told Robert, trying to sound casual. "But she was with a different guy."

"She's a bit fickle, cousin Gloria," Robert agreed. "She's dated every fellow in the U.K. with a drop of noble blood in his veins—this is the second time she's toyed with poor Burton."

Jessica's eyes darted around the room, dazzled by the designer-original dresses, the jewels, the general air of sophistication and gentility. Suddenly, it seemed completely improbable that Lord Robert Pembroke would want to date someone like her—an uncouth, untitled American nobody.

Maybe he's already dated every girl in the U.K. with a drop of noble blood, Jessica speculated. *Maybe he's just toying with me, just for tonight.*

But as Robert whisked her onto the dance floor, his muscular arms wrapped tightly around her waist, Jessica decided she didn't care. One magical night with Lord Robert Pembroke would be enough to last her for the rest of her life.

"When the song is over, I'll introduce you to Lady Amanda and Lord Charles Darlington." Twirling her, Robert nodded toward a group of people chatting and laughing nearby. "They're the two redheads, brother and sister, and jolly good company. And I bet you'd adore Lady Catherine Rangeley and her current flame, Neddy. He's a duke, you know."

Jessica burst out laughing and Robert's lips twisted in a wry smile. "You think it's silly and pretentious, don't you, this antiquated social system of ours?"

"Oh, no," Jessica assured him. "I was just imagining how it would translate back home at Sweet Valley High, if all my friends from school had titles. Lord Winston Egbert! And Lady Maria and Lady Amy, and of course *Lila* would insist on being queen." She dimpled mischievously. "I could be the Countess of Calico Drive."

"You'd make a splendid countess," Robert declared, dipping her backward, tango style. "But you're probably better off the way you are. I actually envy you equality-minded, unstuffy Americans."

Jessica raised her eyebrows. "You can't tell me you don't like being a lord!"

"It has its advantages, of course, and I shamelessly make the most of them," he conceded with a

117

rakish smile. "There *are* times, though, when the expectations are downright inconvenient and inhibiting. Take school, for example. I was packed off to Eaton as a boy, like my father and every male Pembroke before me, even though anyone could have predicted that I was primed for rebellion. It was an utter disaster. I was expelled from a grand total of six of the finest schools in England before I ended up in one that wasn't full of overbred, conformist, gutless ninnies."

Jessica laughed. "You would like Sweet Valley High, then. There are a few ninnies, but lots of other types of people, too."

Robert grinned. "I could have been a California surfer instead of an English lord. What a concept!"

"So, what exactly does an English lord *do*?" asked Jessica as they stepped apart to dance to a fast tune.

"Now, that's a good question, and you'd get a different answer from my father. *He* feels that each successive Lord Pembroke should live exactly like the one before him. Manage the estate and the family business interests in the most conservative manner possible, marry the richest and most boring girl you can find, and in general keep up the good old Pembroke name."

Jessica recalled her conversation with Tony at the *Journal*. "But you have different ideas."

Robert smiled. "A few."

The tempo of the music slowed, and Robert drew Jessica close once more. She looked up into his cool, sexy gray-blue eyes, her lashes fluttering and her heart giving a telltale thump. *I'm falling in love,* she thought blissfully.

"Tomorrow night . . . are you free?" Robert asked.

Jessica nodded.

"Good. And how about this weekend? I'll be at Pembroke Manor, my family's country seat. It's an easy train ride from London—would you like to join us? Bring your twin sister, and her beau if she has one."

A weekend at Pembroke Manor! Jessica nearly swooned. "I'd love to."

"Grand." Robert gave her a little squeeze. "There's nothing like a canter around the estate on a breezy summer afternoon." His eyes twinkled. "And I know my mother would be delighted to renew her acquaintance with you. Sergeant Bumpo actually managed to recover her mink!"

A weekend at Pembroke Manor . . . As she slow-danced with Robert, Jessica's eyes grew misty with visions of herself riding around the English countryside with Robert. He would want to show her every inch of Pembroke land . . . because someday it would be her home, too. *I'd give up Sweet Valley in a minute. Lady Jessica Pembroke,* she thought with a rapturous sigh. *No doubt about it, it's my destiny!*

Chapter 9

"Elizabeth, there you are."

Elizabeth looked up from *Dr. Jekyll and Mr. Hyde* to see Mrs. Bates beckoning to her from the door to the library. "You have a call on the hall telephone. Long distance from America."

Mom and Dad! Elizabeth thought. Tossing the book aside, she sprinted to the phone where she'd seen Portia talking earlier. "Hello?"

"Liz, it's Todd."

"Todd!" Elizabeth nearly dropped the receiver. "Todd," she repeated. "It's you!"

Todd's laugh crackled warmly over the line. "It's me, all right. How are you? How's London? How's the internship?"

"Oh, it's all wonderful. I was going to write you a letter tonight. . . . I can't believe you called! It's so expensive to call overseas—your parents will kill you when they find out."

"I told them how much I missed you, and they said it was OK," Todd assured her. "As long as I keep it under five minutes."

Elizabeth laughed. "In that case, I'll talk fast." Quickly, she told Todd about HIS, and about Lucy Friday, Tony Frank, Sergeant Bumpo, Henry Reeves, and the mysterious murder of Dr. Neville. "We haven't had a dull moment so far," she concluded. "Guess where Jessica is right now? On a date with someone named *Lord* Robert Pembroke."

"Better her than you," he joked.

"Yeah," said Elizabeth, remembering supper at the Gloucester Arms with Luke and her broken date with Rene.

"Well, I should go." Todd's voice was husky with emotion. "I just had to hear your voice. I miss you so much, Liz."

"I miss you, too," she said, suddenly feeling a rush of love and homesickness. "I hate being so far away from you."

"Don't forget about me, OK?"

"Never," Elizabeth promised. "Bye, Todd."

"Bye, Liz. I love you."

"I love you, too."

Hanging up the phone, she rose and slowly padded down the hall toward the staircase. She'd told Todd just about everything that had happened to her since she'd arrived in London except for the episodes involving Rene and Luke. *I just kind of . . . left them out. Is that as bad as lying?* she wondered.

Mixed feelings battled inside her. *Of course*

Todd wants me to have fun while I'm in London—he wants me to make new friends, and some of them are bound to be boys. There's nothing wrong with that. Even so, Elizabeth knew Todd wouldn't be happy to learn she was going out on dates. And maybe after tonight it wouldn't be hard to stay on a platonic level with Rene, but what about Luke?

Reaching the end of the third-floor hallway, Elizabeth pushed open her bedroom door. For an instant, she found herself wishing desperately that she was home in her own room in Sweet Valley. She wanted to be alone with her thoughts, but there was Portia, sitting at her dressing table in a lavender silk robe with her hair in a turban, removing her eye makeup with a cotton ball.

Without greeting her roommate, Elizabeth flung herself onto her bunk. Portia had made it abundantly clear that she couldn't be bothered with even the most fundamental civilities—there was no point trying to chat with her.

Curling up on her side, Elizabeth hugged her pillow. *Oh, Todd,* she thought, wishing he were there to put his arms around her . . . and obliterate the memory of Luke Shepherd's lips brushing her cheek. . . .

She heaved a deep, heartfelt sigh. Portia glanced up from the mirror. "Is anything the matter?" she inquired.

Elizabeth sat up on the bed. *Is she actually deigning to speak to me?* she wondered, surprised. She didn't know quite how to respond—she wasn't about to expose her innermost feelings to someone

123

as cold and unsympathetic as Portia Albert. "No, nothing's the matter," Elizabeth said. "I guess I'm just a little homesick."

Portia twisted in her chair to look at Elizabeth. "You *are* an awfully long way from California."

"I'm used to talking over my day with my parents, getting their feedback. It's strange not being able to do that. I feel kind of . . . adrift."

Elizabeth hadn't intended to confide in Portia; the words just spilled out. She waited for Portia to make a disparaging remark. Instead, Portia tipped her head to one side, her gray eyes thoughtful. "You have that kind of relationship with your parents? You share things? They take an interest?"

"Sure." Idly, Elizabeth reached for a pair of wire-rimmed eyeglasses that someone, Lina she assumed, had left on the night table. She lifted them to her eyes. To her surprise, they didn't affect her vision at all—the lenses appeared to be clear and nonprescriptive. "They're pretty good parents that way," Elizabeth remarked, putting the glasses back down. "They try to stay in touch with what me and my sister and brother are doing. They both work, and it would be easy to be too busy for that kind of thing—I guess they know they have to make an extra effort to make sure we have dinner together most nights, and do things on weekends and that kind of stuff."

Now it was Portia's turn to heave a wistful sigh. "I thought families like that only existed in the movies."

"There's nothing special about us—we're completely boring and ordinary," Elizabeth assured her. "Not like you. It's so exciting that you're following in your father's footsteps—Sir Montford must be very proud of you!"

Reaching for a jar of face cream, Portia twisted off the lid. "Oh, it's just grand. Maybe someday we'll have a chance to perform together—Shakespeare at the Globe, perhaps, or an American made-for-TV movie."

Portia had reverted back to her usual haughtiness so rapidly, Elizabeth couldn't pinpoint the moment of transition. She stared as Portia turned back to the mirror and began smoothing white face cream on her cheeks and forehead. The mask went back on; Portia became a different person before Elizabeth's very eyes. *Or did I imagine that momentary warmth and sympathy?* Elizabeth wondered, baffled and disappointed.

Elizabeth was just drifting off to sleep when Jessica slipped into the bedroom and dashed over to pounce on her sister's bed. "I'm home!" she whispered loudly.

"I noticed," Elizabeth whispered back.

A shadowy nightgowned figure sat up in the other top bunk. "How was your big date?" whispered Lina.

"Fantastic!" Jessica gushed.

She was so excited, she forgot to whisper. "Would you *please* be *quiet?*" Portia snapped. "Tomorrow is dress rehearsal—I need my beauty sleep."

Jessica had to clap a hand to her mouth to stifle

a giggle. In the dark, she could see Lina doing the same.

"Now that you've woken us all up," whispered Elizabeth, "let's go downstairs and raid the refrigerator. C'mon, Lina!"

A minute later, the three girls were tiptoeing down the dark stairs, Elizabeth and Lina in their nightgowns and Jessica still in the dress she'd worn for her date with Robert. They crossed the foyer holding their breath. When Jessica tripped on the rug in the hall outside of Mrs. Bates's apartment, all three of them burst into hysterical laughter.

"Ssh!" Elizabeth hissed. "If she catches us, we're doomed."

"No, listen." Lina held up a hand, her head tipped.

In the silence, Jessica could hear the distant sound of someone snoring. Another giggle tickled her throat. "She sounds like a snuffling old bear."

Lina grinned. "I don't think she heard us—how could she, making all that racket herself?"

In the kitchen, they scrounged up a loaf of homemade raisin bread, some cold roast chicken, and three ripe pears and then sat down at a table in the dark dining room to eat. "I don't know how I can be hungry," Jessica commented as she bit into a sweet, juicy pear. "Robert and I totally pigged out at this fabulous French place, Le Mouton Noir."

"That's one of the finest restaurants in London," said Lina. "He must really be trying to impress you."

"Lord Robert Pembroke doesn't have to *try* to

impress anybody," said Jessica. "For your information, it comes naturally."

Elizabeth snorted. "You mean, it comes with being a rich and pampered aristocrat!"

"Have it your way, Liz. But it just so happens that Robert has very kindly invited both of us for a weekend in the country at Pembroke Manor. He *even* said *you* could bring a date. *If* you can scrape one up."

"A weekend in the country—how delightful!" said Lina. "You should take him up on the offer, Elizabeth. Pembroke Manor is quite a showplace . . . or so I've heard."

"They have an ancestral castle and tons of land and a whole stable full of thoroughbred horses," Jessica confirmed. "Although maybe you wouldn't stoop to ride the horse of a rich and pampered aristocrat."

Elizabeth bit into a piece of raisin bread, smiling. "I'd consider it."

Jessica had a brilliant thought. "Why don't you bring Rene?" she suggested. "He's very sophisticated—I'm sure he'd pass muster with the Pembrokes."

"And that's all that matters," Elizabeth said dryly. "Well, to tell you the truth, I don't see me and Rene spending a weekend together anytime soon." She told Jessica and Lina about spacing out her dinner date with Rene, and his reaction when he saw her come in with Luke.

"Luke? That boring poet guy from work?" When Elizabeth's face turned red as a beet, Jessica pounced. "What happened? Did he kiss you?"

"Not really . . . well, sort of," Elizabeth confessed.

"Well, then, I suppose you could bring Luke," Jessica said. "I mean, Rene would be better . . . Luke's kind of a nobody. . . . You really should be nicer to Rene, Elizabeth."

"Thanks for the advice," Elizabeth said. "But I don't plan to bring Rene *or* Luke anywhere, least of all to Pembroke Manor. Why would I want to spend a weekend at the home of total strangers? And what about you? You hardly know this guy. What would Mom and Dad say?"

Jessica nibbled delicately on a roasted chicken wing. "I'll call them and ask them, but I'm sure they won't mind. Robert's parents will be there, naturally—we'll be chaperoned. And Robert's a perfect gentleman—it's not like he's some bum I picked up on the street. All you have to do is look at him to know what kind of person he is! The way he dresses, the way he speaks, his manners . . ."

"Being rich doesn't automatically make you a good person, any more than being poor makes you a bad person," Elizabeth pointed out. "If you ask me, Robert Pembroke sounds like a conceited, insufferable prig, and he had you wrapped around his finger in under ten seconds simply because he puts the word 'Lord' in front of his name."

Lina had been listening to this exchange with an amused smile. "Oh, Rob's not a bad sort," she interjected.

Both Jessica and Elizabeth shot Lina a look as if to ask, *How would* you *know?*

"What I mean is, he doesn't *appear* to be a bad sort," Lila amended. "He doesn't make it into the gossip columns nearly as often as *some* of the spoiled young gentry in this town."

Jessica flashed a triumphant smile. "See, Liz? Face it, you're just jealous. But I'll tell you one thing right now. Nothing, and I mean *nothing*, is going to keep me away from Pembroke Manor this weekend!"

Having polished off their midnight snack, the three girls tiptoed back upstairs. Lina made a detour to the bathroom and Jessica and Elizabeth crawled into their bunks. With Portia snoring softly, it seemed safe to whisper.

"Jess, do you think there's anything . . . funny about Lina?" Elizabeth asked.

Jessica hung over the edge of the bed and looked down at her sister. "What do you mean?"

"I mean . . ." Elizabeth couldn't really put her finger on what it was about her new friend that didn't seem quite right. Was it the eyeglasses? Something Lina had said? "Take the nightgown she's wearing tonight. With all that fancy lace—it must have been expensive."

"Just because you're poor doesn't mean you can't have a few nice things," Jessica pointed out, reluctant to mention the dress she and Emily had found in the back of the closet. "Maybe somebody gave it to her."

"Maybe."

"If you ask me, the only thing odd about Lina is

that she could be a knockout if she tried," remarked Jessica. "You don't have to have a lot of money to have style—it's almost like she goes out of her way to be dowdy."

"Hmm." Elizabeth plumped up her pillow and changed the subject. "I told Luke about how Dr. Neville died, Jessica, and about Lord Pembroke and the police chief being at the scene of the murder when Lucy was reporting it, and Lucy quitting because of a cover-up. And he thinks . . . Dr. Neville's murder, and Poo-Poo's . . . Luke thinks it might be the work of a werewolf."

"A werewolf?" Jessica burst out laughing. "Liz, I was just *kidding* when I said that. Honestly, I think all that poetry has addled both your brains!"

"Something very strange is going on," Elizabeth insisted, "and Lord Pembroke Senior knows what it is and he's making Henry Reeves and the police department hush up about it."

"The Pembrokes have nothing to do with the murder or any cover-up," Jessica declared hotly. "It's just a coincidence that Lord P. Senior owns the *Journal* and was friends with Dr. Neville—it doesn't make him guilty of anything. You're jumping to conclusions in the worst way, Liz, and I think it's very unfair."

"Well . . ." Her sister had a point. Still, Elizabeth wasn't quite ready to trust the Pembrokes. "Have you talked to Robert about the murder, and what—who—we saw at Dr. Neville's flat?"

"No," said Jessica. "It didn't come up tonight, either."

"Don't mention it, then. Not until we've had a chance to do more sleuthing and find out what's really going on at the *Journal*. It's possible that Lucy could be wrong, that things don't add up the way she thinks they do."

Suddenly, Jessica's eyes lit up, gleaming in the dark. "Remember what Lucy said to Tony, though, about this not being the first time, or something like that? Werewolf or not, maybe other murders have been covered up or played down!"

"That would explain why Lucy got so mad about this one," Elizabeth agreed.

"First thing tomorrow, then," Jessica proposed, "let's find out!"

Arriving at the *London Journal* offices half an hour early on Wednesday morning, the twins hurried straight to the research department. The large, cluttered room was unoccupied. "Good," said Elizabeth, sitting down at a microfiche machine. "I'd just as soon not have to explain to anybody what we're doing."

"You mean, you'd just as soon not have to lie," said Jessica.

Elizabeth grinned. "Right."

Jessica scanned the microfiche index. "They have copies of the *Journal* going back about a thousand years," she announced. "How far back should we look?"

"Let's start with recent issues—the last month, say. If we don't find anything, we can go back further."

With Jessica looking eagerly over her shoulder,

Elizabeth twirled the knob of the microfiche machine. Past issues of the *Journal* rolled across the screen, the print very tiny. After skimming a week's worth of "Crime Reporter" columns to no avail, Jessica suddenly cried out. "How 'bout that one: 'Man Found in Park, Dead of Multiple Stab Wounds?'"

"It's a pretty straightforward case, though," Elizabeth pointed out. "He was mugged and stabbed a bunch of times. It's horrible, but not mysterious. They lay the facts right out. We're looking for something that's *not* there, remember?"

"Right. Keep rolling."

They'd pored over three weeks of London crime when Elizabeth caught her breath sharply. "Take a look at this one," she commanded Jessica. "The blurb at the bottom of the page."

Jessica read the brief headline: "Nurse Dies on the Job." She nodded, her eyes moving quickly to the end of the short article. "It reminds me of the story they printed about Dr. Neville, the way it's so vague about how she actually died. They say it was a robbery, but did the attacker stab her, shoot her, bludgeon her?"

"It could definitely be another cover-up," Elizabeth asserted. "We have to talk to Lucy about it."

"Easier said than done," Jessica reminded her sister as they left the research department and headed toward Tony's office to get the day's assignment. "She quit, remember?"

"We'll just have to call or visit her at home. Maybe Tony knows where she lives."

"But what if they get mad?" said Jessica. "Tony

and Lucy, I mean. We'll have to tell them we were sneaking around at Dr. Neville's when we were supposed to be keeping out of trouble with Sergeant Bumpo!"

"I'm sure they'll overlook it—it's a pretty small crime compared to murder," Elizabeth reasoned. "Or to covering up a murder."

Rounding a corner, they nearly collided with Luke. "Good morning," he said, his cheeks turning faintly pink as he smiled at Elizabeth. "Where are you off to in such a rush?"

Elizabeth glanced at Jessica. "I think we should tell him. We may need his help."

Jessica shrugged. She was peeved with Luke for casting aspersions on the integrity of the Pembroke family, but in general he was bland and harmless enough. *If Liz wants to bring her little crush along for the ride, fine with me.* "Whatever."

"Tell me what?" asked Luke.

Elizabeth filled him in on their microfiche discovery. "You're onto something," he agreed, his blue eyes blazing. "And Lucy Friday may very well hold the key to the puzzle."

Brimming with purpose, the three charged over to Tony's desk. Elizabeth cleared her throat. "Tony, we need to talk to you about something important."

He raised his sandy eyebrows. "I'm all ears."

"It's about . . . Dr. Neville's murder," she explained.

Tony sat up in his chair. "What *about* Dr. Neville's murder?"

"Well, we know Lucy quit because Reeves didn't print her story of what really happened. And we know what really happened because . . . we were there."

Tony looked both puzzled and astonished. "You were *where*?"

"At Dr. Neville's townhouse," Elizabeth confessed.

"Looking in the window," Jessica elaborated.

"The girls saw the body," Luke offered.

"And we heard Lucy describe its . . . condition," Elizabeth finished.

Tony whistled. "And all that time, Lucy thought you were safe with our man Bumpo!"

Relieved that Tony didn't appear angry, Elizabeth forged ahead. "We also saw two men at the scene with Lucy—Lord Robert Pembroke, who owns this newspaper, and Andrew Thatcher, the London chief of police. So we think that maybe they were in on the decision to suppress the true facts of Dr. Neville's death. Now we need to find out *why* anyone would want to do that, and we think we've found a clue—a connection to another murder that took place about a month ago. We need to speak to Lucy."

Tony shook his head. "It all sounds a bit wiggy to me. But I know Lucy sincerely believes something is amiss here at the paper. She felt strongly enough about it to quit her post." Rising to his feet, he reached for his rumpled tweed jacket. "She'd want to hear what you have to say. Come along—I'll take you to her."

Tony had to press the doorbell at Lucy's flat

134

three times before they heard the sound of approaching footsteps. A bolt rattled and the door swung open.

Lucy gazed out, her hazel eyes widening. "Frank! Twins! Luke!" she exclaimed, startled. "What brings you here?"

"I'm just the chauffeur," Tony said. "The children have something urgent to discuss with you."

Lucy escorted them into her parlor, which was decorated with antiques and potted plants. When they were all seated, Elizabeth went straight to the point, talking fast. "We know you quit because Reeves didn't print your story about Dr. Neville, and we know what was in your story because we were at the scene, looking in the window, and saw the body and heard you speaking into your tape recorder. We did some research and came upon an article about a murdered nurse. Can you tell us if Nurse Handley's body was . . . mangled like Dr. Neville's?"

Lucy stared in disbelief at Elizabeth. "You picked up on the Handley case? You'll make darn good reporters." She drummed her fingers on the arm of her chair. "Yes," she said, after a long, pregnant pause. "Nurse Handley died in the same way that Dr. Neville did. She was savagely attacked— her throat was ripped open and she bled to death."

Elizabeth gasped, putting a hand to her own throat. Jessica and Luke both blanched, and even sensible Tony looked spooked.

"The crimes appeared very similar," Lucy continued. "Serial killers tend to have a distinctive signature, and for this one, it's the clawed, mutilated throat."

"Serial killers?" squeaked Jessica.

Lucy nodded. "A serial killer is on the loose. There's no question about it. I know the police and Scotland Yard have come to the same conclusion, but for some reason they're keeping quiet. They're dragging their feet . . . on *someone's* orders."

A stunned silence fell over the room. Goose bumps prickled up and down Elizabeth's arms. A serial killer . . . *Dr. Neville wasn't the only victim. There have been multiple killings, with more to come. Maybe Luke is right about the werewolf. . . .*

"They may be keeping quiet so as not to panic the public," Tony suggested reasonably.

Lucy's eyes flashed. "The public has a right to know! How else can people protect themselves?"

Elizabeth shivered, remembering Poo-Poo. Someone had killed him, too. Someone . . . or something . . . that might still have been lurking in the shadows when Elizabeth and Lina discovered the poor dog's body.

"Remember Lady Wimpole's missing Yorkie?" Elizabeth asked Lucy. "Did you read in yesterday's 'Crime Reporter' about how I stumbled across his body . . . dead, with his throat ripped out?"

Lucy's expression grew even darker. "It's a serial killer," she repeated. "And perhaps one of the most heinous ever to walk the night streets of London. Is there a method to how he—or she—chooses his victims, or does he simply lose control?"

For some reason, words Luke had uttered at

the wax museum suddenly flickered through Elizabeth's brain. *"We all have an animal side, Elizabeth. . . ."*

"Do you think Lord Pembroke, the owner of the *Journal*, could have anything to do with the cover-up?" wondered Luke.

Lucy pushed back her hair, looking thoughtful. "Hmm . . . the silver cigarette case," she murmured.

"The one Lord Pembroke was holding?" asked Elizabeth.

"It was found by the body," said Lucy, "and it was engraved with the intials R.H.P., the Lord's own initials—or those of his son."

Elizabeth and Luke exchanged a meaningful glance. "The only other idea we've had," she said, "is that Reeves may have played up the sensational Princess Eliana headlines to deflect notice from Dr. Neville's murder. What do you think about that?"

"I hadn't considered that angle, but it makes sense, especially if Reeves is trying to compete with the *Post*—"

Tony had been listening to the conversation with an anxious look on his face. Now he jumped up from his seat and cut Lucy off with a sharp gesture. "Friday, really," he reprimanded her. "Ought you to discuss confidential details of such sensitive cases with our teenaged summer interns? We don't know anything for sure. The cover-up is just speculation, and in all propriety we shouldn't presume—"

"Just speculation?" Lucy burst out. "All propriety? Balderdash, Frank. Don't you trust my judgment? Of course there's a cover-up, and Reeves and the police department are behind it, and perhaps Pembroke is behind *them!*"

Suddenly, her eyes narrowed suspiciously. "And what about *you*, Frank? You've been getting pretty tight with Reeves lately." Tears of anger and disappointment sprang into her eyes. "I thought you were— But you've always wanted my job, haven't you? You never thought a woman could handle it. Are you part of the cover-up, too, Frank? Did you see this coming, that I'd quit over it? Did Reeves promise you the crime desk if you took his side against me?"

"How dare you accuse me of such underhanded tactics!" Tony exploded. "I'm not taking Reeves's side—I'm not taking anyone's side! I'm merely attempting to be rational and objective in the interest of good journalism and basic human justice."

"In the interest of climbing the *London Journal* ladder and feathering your own nest, you mean!" Lucy countered hotly.

The twins and Luke gaped. "You're way out of line, Miss Friday," Tony said hoarsely.

"And so are you, Mr. Frank," she shouted. She pointed toward the door, her eyes shooting sparks. "Get out of my house this minute. I never want to see you again!"

Chapter 10

Jessica, Elizabeth, and Luke quickly said an embarrassed good-bye to Lucy, who was so agitated she didn't even seem to hear them. Hurrying out to the sidewalk, they looked in both directions, but Tony, and his car, had disappeared from sight.

"Looks like we're hoofing it back to work," Luke observed. "What a row *that* was!"

"Poor Lucy," said Elizabeth.

"Poor Tony!" said Jessica.

Slowly, the three began walking in the direction of the *London Journal* offices. "So, where do we go from here?" wondered Luke.

"I'm still totally confused," Elizabeth confessed. "The evidence points to the same person killing both Dr. Neville and Nurse Handley, but is there a connection between the victims or is the murderer's choice just random? Is it important that the silver cigarette case belonged to a Pembroke?

What motive could Lord Pembroke, Chief Thatcher, and Henry Reeves have for conspiring to suppress the facts of the case?"

"We have more questions than ever," Luke agreed.

"Well, *I* don't," Jessica piped in. "I don't think you can lump Lord Pembroke in with Thatcher and Reeves—there's just no way he has anything to do with a cover-up." Her blue-green eyes flashed indignantly. "I mean, really! The Pembrokes are one of the most prominent families in England— they're the *nobility*."

"That doesn't automatically put them above suspicion," argued Elizabeth.

"It does in my opinion," Jessica insisted. "You're barking up the wrong tree, Liz. If you want to find some crooks and killers, start looking in the lower classes."

Luke clenched his jaw. "The aristocracy manage, in their own fashion, to commit just as many crimes as the rest of us," he said stiffly. "And they probably get away with them more often."

"I think we can agree on one thing," Elizabeth intervened. "Two people and a dog have been brutally killed, and the newspapers and police department are hushing it up. Something nasty is going on." She looked at her sister, her eyes flashing a challenge. "So, are we going to crack this case together?"

Jessica nodded. "You bet. If only to prove that you're wrong about the Pembrokes!"

"I think that's enough scones," Lina said with a

laugh. "I count at least a dozen and half, and we're only five people!"

Elizabeth, Lina, Emily, David, and Gabriello were roaming the food courts at Harrod's, London's largest department store, buying sweets for a late-afternoon picnic tea in the park. "But there are so many different flavors, and they all sound so delicious," said Elizabeth. "Did we get any of these orange-currant scones?"

"Plain is fine for me," announced Emily, holding up a carton of Devonshire cream and a jar of jam. "I plan to drown mine in cream and jam, anyway!"

"And don't forget, we have cookies." David displayed a bulging paper sack. "This should tide us over until dinner."

After paying for their selections, the HIS group crossed the street and entered the cool green oasis of Hyde Park. Gabriello pulled a blanket from his rucksack and spread it out on the grass under a spreading oak tree. All five dropped down and reached for the bags of scones and cookies.

"This is the life," remarked Emily, topping a plump scone with a generous dollop of cream.

Elizabeth sighed rapturously, her eyes on an equestrian cantering past on the bridle trail. "I think London must be the most beautiful city in the world."

"Then you haven't been to Florence or Rome," said Gabriello with a wink.

"London's not so bad," David agreed in his soft Liverpudlian accent. He cast a shy glance in Lina's direction. "Though it's too big and fancy to have the charm of Liverpool, eh, Lina?"

141

She shrugged, not replying.

"It's funny, though, what people think about Liverpool." David shook his head, grinning. "There are two Americans in my program at the university, Zack and Kelly, and of course the only thing they'd ever heard about Liverpool is that the Beatles came from there. They asked me if I'd known John, Paul, Ringo, and George."

Elizabeth laughed. "Even though you weren't even *born* when the band was together in the sixties!"

"Right. I pointed that out. So, you know how there was a fifth Beatle, another drummer before Ringo? Well, just for a laugh, I told the Americans that my father had been the *sixth* Beatle—the drummer *before* the drummer before Ringo. I was joking, of course. But they actually fell for it. 'Ah, that's right, the legendary sixth Beatle,' Zack said." David mimicked a flat-voweled American twang. "'I always *wondered* who that was!'"

Elizabeth, Emily, and Gabriello burst out laughing. Lina's lips twitched as if she were trying hard not to smile.

"Not all Americans are so ridiculous," said Elizabeth. "But I'll admit I don't know much about Liverpool."

"You should visit," David urged her. "Shouldn't she, Lina?"

Lina shifted restlessly on the blanket. "Certainly, if she wants." Abruptly, she sprang to her feet. "Let's feed these extra scones to the ducks, shall we?"

Lina, Gabriello, and Emily strolled to a nearby pond, which sparkled like gold in the last rays of the sun. Elizabeth and David watched them toss crumbs to the birds that flocked over, clamoring loudly.

"I'm a bumbler, I am," David muttered after a moment, glancing shyly at Elizabeth out of the corner of his eye. "The harder I try to make her notice me, the more she turns and looks the other way."

It wasn't difficult for Elizabeth to guess that he was talking about Lina. "She does come across as a little . . . standoffish," she had to agree.

David pulled his knees up to his chin and sighed glumly. "The thing is, I really like her," he confided. "I'd like to ask her out. But just when I think I'm finally making a connection, she runs away like a frightened deer."

Elizabeth shook her head thoughtfully. "She's a puzzle. Because I get the impression she likes you, too, though she won't admit it. I guess . . ." Elizabeth offered the obvious explanation, even though it didn't quite satisfy her. "I guess she's just shy. It might take a while, but I bet you'll get through to her one of these days."

"Do you really think so?" David's eyes glowed with hope. "Do you think . . . do you think you could help me, Elizabeth? Put in a good word?"

Elizabeth smiled. David and Lina *would* make the sweetest couple. And helping along their romance might be a nice change from tracking down a serial killer. . . . "Sure. I'll put in a good word. We'll find a way to get you two together, just wait and see!"

*　　*　　*

"I can't believe Portia's already up and gone," said Lina on Thursday morning as she and the twins dressed for work. "She's slept late every day we've roomed together."

"Tonight's opening night, right?" Jessica grinned wickedly. "She probably went someplace else to get her beauty sleep, because we always make so much noise."

Sliding a headband into her hair, Elizabeth stepped over to her dressing table to see how it looked. Someone had propped an envelope on the table—Elizabeth recognized Portia's bold, flowery script. "Look, it's addressed to the three of us, from Portia!"

"What's in it?" asked Jessica.

"Poison, I bet, or explosives," kidded Lina.

Elizabeth opened the envelope and drew out a bunch of theater tickets. "Tickets to the opening-night performance of *A Common Man*," she said in disbelief. "Seven of them! *And* an invitation backstage after the performance."

Lina blinked through her wire-rimmed glasses. "You're joshing!"

"Not at all. There's a note, too." Elizabeth read it out loud. "'Elizabeth, Jessica, and Lina, I'd be very pleased if you would attend my West End debut this evening, as my special guests. I'm enclosing tickets for Emily, Rene, David, and Gabriello as well. Wish me luck!'"

"She expects us to wish her luck, after the way she's treated us?" Jessica snorted. "Fat chance. 'Break a leg,' maybe—I wouldn't mind if she did!"

"What do you suppose she's up to?" Lina's brow furrowed with suspicion. "Maybe it's a trick—maybe the tickets are fake and we'll go to the theater only to be turned away."

"No, they're real," said Jessica. "She's showing off—she wants us to see what a big star she is so she can gloat endlessly."

"Either way, I say we boycott *A Common Man*," Lina declared. "I bet the others will agree."

Elizabeth studied Portia's note thoughtfully. There was something very unPortialike about it, something simple and sincere. "I don't think she's showing off or trying to trick us," Elizabeth disagreed. "Maybe the tickets are just a friendly, generous gesture."

"I doubt that," Jessica said disparagingly.

"We won't know unless we go to the play," Elizabeth concluded. "What harm will it do us to give Portia one last chance?"

Since the morning was sunny and beautiful, Jessica and Elizabeth decided to walk an extra half mile before getting on the tube. "There's a station near Buckingham Palace," Elizabeth recalled. "We can watch the changing of the queen's guard."

Despite the early hour, quite a few tourists had gathered to observe the pomp and circumstance of red-uniformed guards on shiny black horses parading in front of the royal residence. "Those hats kill me," said Jessica, pointing to one of the tall beaver hats. "And why don't they wear the chin straps under their chins where they belong?"

Elizabeth pondered other questions as the dignified guards trotted by. "A lot of people work awfully hard to safeguard the queen and her family," she mused. "How did anyone manage to get to Princess Eliana and steal her away?"

"I wonder if they'll ever find her." Jessica crossed her arms, shivering. "Maybe they won't find her until she's dead. Maybe the serial killer has gotten her!"

"Jess, you have the sickest imagination," Elizabeth exclaimed, but the same possibility, however unlikely, had occurred to her, too.

Jessica tossed a final, wistful glance over her shoulder at Buckingham Palace as they headed toward the tube station. "It must be amazing to live there," she said. "And to think we have a chance to visit someplace *almost* as cool—Pembroke Manor!"

"I told you the other night, I'm not interested in spending a weekend with the Pembrokes," Elizabeth reminded her sister.

"Please, Elizabeth?" Jessica wheedled. "It will be a blast, I swear. It could even be educational— you'll get to see another part of England, with lots of old historical stuff."

"I'd rather take a day trip to Oxford or Cambridge."

Jessica hung on Elizabeth's arm. "But Mom and Dad said I can only go if you go, too, and I'll just *die* if I don't go," she wailed melodramatically. "Robert said you could bring Luke, remember? Don't you want to spend some time with him, since you have such a crush on him? Please, please, *please*."

Elizabeth kept Jessica in suspense for a good long minute. "OK," she said at last. "I'll come, and I'll ask Luke. At least then I'd have someone normal to talk to."

"I knew you'd come around." Jessica gave her sister a hug. "You're going to just love the Pembrokes!"

Elizabeth doubted that, but she didn't say so. Jessica had hit on one tactic to get Elizabeth to change her mind about going to Pembroke Manor: her growing romantic interest in Luke Shepherd. But there was another, equally compelling reason for her decision.

I don't expect to love the Pembrokes, Elizabeth thought as she and Jessica boarded the tube, *but maybe I'll learn something about them that will help me solve the mystery of the murder cover-up!*

"We need a plan of action," Luke declared as he and Elizabeth huddled over cups of tea at his desk in the corner of the *Journal* offices. "If there's a cover-up taking place—and we both agree with Lucy that there is—we need to uncover it. But how?"

"Let's go over what we know and don't know," Elizabeth suggested, grabbing a pen and paper so she could make a list. "We know that Dr. Neville was murdered last Sunday night by someone—or something—that tore his throat out. Approximately twenty-four hours later, Lady Wimpole's dog was dispatched of in much the same manner. But it started a month ago, with the murder of Nurse Handley. We have three bodies."

"Both Nurse Handley's and Dr. Neville's deaths were downplayed in the *Journal*, apparently on the orders of Henry Reeves, the editor-in-chief," Luke contributed.

"We suspect, but we don't know for certain, that Lord Robert Pembroke, owner of the *Journal* and father of the guy my insane sister is currently dating, may have dictated Reeves's editorial decision. Pembroke was at the scene of the crime when Lucy went to report it, as was Andrew Thatcher, the London chief of police. To the best of our knowledge, Pembroke is acquainted with all the key players, dead and alive, except the nurse and Poo-Poo, of course."

"And there's that cigarette case. . . . Yes, he's the crucial link," Luke agreed. He raked a hand through his mop of glossy dark hair. "Now, what we *don't* know . . ."

Elizabeth ticked off the items on her fingers. "The identity of the murderer. The motives for the murders, and the link, if any, between the victims. The motive for the cover-up. Are Pembroke and Reeves and the police protecting someone? Do they have a suspect?"

"We've got a long way to go," Luke remarked, sitting back in his chair and folding his hands behind his neck.

Elizabeth sipped her tea. "A long way. But I've thought of a place we could start. Pembroke Manor."

Luke's dark eyebrows shot up. "Pembroke Manor?"

Elizabeth nodded. "Robert Junior invited Jessica up to the country for the weekend. I'm invited, too, and I can bring a date." Warmth flooded Elizabeth's cheeks, and she dropped her eyes, wondering if Luke would detect how nervous and excited she was at the thought of going off for a weekend with him. "Would you—would you like to come with us?"

"Yes."

Elizabeth glanced up in surprise at Luke's rapid response. There was a strangely intense and yet faraway look in his eyes, and suddenly she remembered what she'd said to Jessica a few nights ago: "How well do you know Robert Pembroke? Do you really want to spend a weekend in some remote, isolated place with a perfect stranger?"

I don't know Luke any better than Jessica knows Robert, Elizabeth thought, momentarily disconcerted. *How did we come to be so involved with this whole mystery . . . and with each other . . . in just three days?*

"Yes, I'll come with you," Luke repeated. He put a hand on Elizabeth's, and a warm, electric tingle shot up her arm. "Just think of the sleuthing possibilities!"

Elizabeth smiled. "Right. How better to learn about the Pembroke family, and their secrets, than by staying in their home?"

Chapter 11

"It's the weekend!" Jessica exulted as she, Elizabeth, and Luke dashed out of the *London Journal* office building late Thursday afternoon. "For us, anyway."

"Tony was really nice to give us tomorrow off so we can have an extra day at Pembroke Manor," said Elizabeth.

"It's the least he could do, seeing as how he's still making us tag after Sergeant Bumpo." Jessica rolled her eyes. "We thought we'd get a break, now that Reeves has put Tony in charge of the crime desk temporarily," she explained to Luke. "Maybe we'd get to tackle something hard-core. Real crime, you know? No such luck."

"Tony decided that we'd been doing such a good job covering Bumpo's beat, we should stick with it." Elizabeth laughed. "So off we went to look into what Jessica dubbed 'The Case of the Exploding Eggplant.'"

Luke grinned. "Sounds like something Holmes himself would have hesitated to take on."

"Can you walk partway home with us?" Elizabeth asked.

"Nothing would give me more pleasure," said Luke. "Shall we go by way of Piccadilly Circus and Carnaby Street? I bet you haven't been there yet."

As they strolled the tree-lined, sun-dappled streets, bombarded by a cheerful cacophony of city sounds, Jessica related their latest Bumpo misadventure. "It was probably the biggest case to challenge Scotland Yard in decades," she began solemnly. "A vendor at the farmer's market had complained that some of his produce was, er, exploding."

"Exploding," Luke repeated, one eyebrow lifting skeptically.

"First a melon." Jessica spread her arms. "Kabam. Then a bushel of tomatoes. Ker-plooey. It was a mess! And not too good for business—who wants to buy exploding veggies? Enter Sergeant Benjamin Bumpo, the pride of Scotland Yard."

Elizabeth giggled, remembering. "He looked so dapper and professional—you could tell his suit had just been pressed. And his hair—what's left of it—was combed oh so carefully over his bald spot. Every strand in place."

"We arrived at the scene just as he did," Jessica continued. "So, there's ol' Bumpo talking to McDivitt, the produce vendor, when all of a sudden, out of nowhere . . ."

"Ka-bam?" Luke guessed.

Jessica nodded. "A dozen heads . . . of lettuce

152

went flying. One shot right by Bumpo like a cannonball. You should have seen his expression!"

Elizabeth picked up the tale. "A few seconds later, on the other side of the cart, a big purple eggplant exploded. Bumpo went to investigate. And just as he was leaning over the bin . . ."

"Ker-plooey?" said Luke.

"Another eggplant detonated right in his face," Jessica confirmed. "Seeds and pulp spattered all over his nice suit, and a big slab of purple eggplant skin ended up draped on top of his head like a toupee. I have never, *ever* laughed so hard."

"Poor Bumpo." Elizabeth wiped tears of laughter from her eyes. "He should really ask for a desk job."

"Well, did he solve the crime?" asked Luke as they turned onto Carnaby Street.

"To his credit, he did," said Elizabeth. "It turned out another vendor at the farmer's market thought McDivitt was encroaching on his turf, and undercutting his prices to boot. He planted little firecrackers in the fruits and vegetables to try to scare McDivitt off."

"But he didn't reckon on Bumpo of the Yard," concluded Jessica.

They all laughed as they continued up Carnaby Street, window-shopping and people-watching. "I've never seen so much black leather," Elizabeth whispered. "And the hairdos!"

All three turned to stare after a young man with a foot-high, neon-green Mohawk. "His ear must have been pierced ten times," Jessica marveled.

She stopped to thumb through a rack of gauzy "grunge" dresses. "How 'bout it, Liz? Want to give Mom and Dad a scare, and arrive home wearing clothes like this and with our hair dyed five different colors?"

"And some studded leather accessories and skull-and-crossbone jewelry," Elizabeth suggested.

To Jessica's disappointment, Piccadilly Circus wasn't a circus at all. "It's just shops and cinemas," she observed.

"We use the word differently in Britain," Luke confirmed. "A circus is a big, open place where a bunch of streets intersect. There's usually a market of some kind. They do have street performers in Piccadilly, though. Look at the clown selling balloons!"

They browsed the stalls, Jessica buying a silk scarf and Elizabeth emptying her pockets of change to purchase a beautiful used leather-bound copy of *Wuthering Heights*. "We should probably head home, Jess," Elizabeth said after half an hour. "Don't forget, we're seeing Portia's play tonight."

"Just one more thing," Jessica begged. She dragged Elizabeth and Luke over to a stall draped with rainbow-colored curtains. "A gypsy fortune-teller. I want to get my palm read!"

"You don't really believe in that stuff, do you?" scoffed Elizabeth.

"Well, that depends." Jessica grinned. "If she tells me I'm going to marry a tall, dark-haired British nobleman with the initials R.H.P., I'll believe!"

The gypsy was an unbelievably ancient woman with a dried-apple face and a turban decorated with tiny silver-and-gold stars and planets. She gestured with one withered, clawlike hand and Jessica sat down in the chair next to her, Elizabeth and Luke standing at a polite distance.

"I want to know what my future holds," said Jessica, extending her hand with the palm facing up.

The gypsy took Jessica's hand, smoothing it flat. As she traced the lines with her own gnarled index finger, her lips moved in some kind of incantation. "What's she saying?" Elizabeth whispered to Luke.

"I can't tell," he whispered back.

Suddenly, the gypsy froze, her wrinkled cheeks growing pale as she stared down at Jessica's palm. "Beware the full moon," she croaked, closing Jessica's hand into a fist. "Beware the full moon."

"Is that all?" Jessica asked in surprise when the gypsy dropped her hand and took a step backward.

"Geez, what a rip-off," she muttered indignantly as she rejoined Luke and Elizabeth. "I thought she was going to tell me all about my future—what my career would be, who I'd marry, how many kids I'd have, stuff like that. 'Beware the full moon'—what kind of dumb fortune is that?"

Elizabeth and Luke exchanged a worried glance. "It's the same thing the bag lady said the day we arrived in London," Elizabeth reminded Jessica. "It's what the villagers said to the boys in *An American Werewolf in London*."

"I know, isn't it hysterical?" Jessica laughed. "Maybe it's the same old lady—she must have seen the movie!"

Somehow, Elizabeth couldn't bring herself to

laugh. Somehow, she couldn't see it as a harmless coincidence. She looked at Luke, and found her own apprehension mirrored in his somber eyes. *We're both thinking about the same thing,* she realized. *The murders . . . and the killer, still at large . . .*

"There's a full moon tomorrow night," Luke told the twins. "You know what that means. . . ."

At HIS, Elizabeth, Jessica, Emily, David, and Gabriello gobbled an early dinner before heading out to the theater.

"Too bad Rene isn't able to come tonight," remarked David. "He has an embassy function, as usual." He lowered his voice. "But where's . . ."

"Lina?" Elizabeth shook her head. "I don't know. Sometimes she gets tied up at the shelter— I'm sure she'll be here any minute. And I'll make sure you two sit next to each other during the play," she whispered with a conspiratorial wink.

When it was time to leave, however, Lina still hadn't appeared. "I'll just check upstairs," Elizabeth offered. "She may have come in while we were eating and gone to the room to change."

She did find Lina in their bedroom. But rather than getting ready to go out, Lina was just making herself comfortable in one of the easy chairs, an afghan wrapped around her knees and a book in her hand.

"Aren't you coming?" Elizabeth asked in surprise.

Lina shook her head. "Portia hasn't had one nice thing to say to me all this time we've shared a room. I had a long day and, frankly, I'd rather spend a pleasant, quiet evening reading than watch her strut about onstage."

"But David will be so disappointed!" Elizabeth exclaimed. Lina turned bright pink and Elizabeth pressed her point. "He's really hoping for a chance to get to know you better."

"He *mustn't* get to know me better!" Lina burst out.

"But I thought you liked him," said Elizabeth, puzzled. "And he likes you. Isn't that good?"

"Definitely not," Lina declared. "Don't you see, Elizabeth? I can't go out with David, and I can't attend opening night at a fashionable West End theater. I just *can't.*"

"Why not?" asked Elizabeth, completely baffled.

"Don't you see?" Lina repeated. She stared at Elizabeth, saying again, "Don't you *see?*"

Elizabeth stared back at Lina. Speaking just now, Lina's voice had altered, her thick Liverpudlian accent giving way to more modulated, elegant tones. There was something different about her expression, too, something almost . . . regal.

Taking off her wire-rimmed glasses, Lina tossed back her cropped brown hair and lifted her delicate chin. "Look at me," she commanded Elizabeth. "Look closely."

Elizabeth did as she was told and suddenly felt a jolt of recognition. *The picture in the newspaper at the airport our first day!* she thought. The hair was shorter and darker, and the glasses were new, and of course the accent was a fake, but the face was the same. . . . "Princess Eliana!" Elizabeth gasped.

157

Eliana heaved a deep, tired sigh. "None other."

Elizabeth's knees buckled as if she'd been kicked from behind. She sank, breathless, into the other armchair. "But how . . . why . . . ? You ran away—you weren't kidnapped at all!"

"I ran away," Eliana confirmed.

"But why?" Elizabeth looked at Eliana's plain white blouse and drab gray sweater and then glanced around the spartan bedroom.

"I know what you're thinking," Eliana said. "Why would anyone give up life in a palace for this? Why would I go from my mother, the Queen of England, to crotchety old Mrs. Bates? From private tutors and charity balls to soup kitchens and homeless shelters?" She lifted her slender shoulders. "I was tired of living behind a fence, like a rare bird in a gilded cage, sheltered and pampered. I wanted to find out what my city was really like. And I wanted to give something back to the world, for once—I've never had to do anything for myself, much less for other people."

"How did you get away?" Elizabeth wondered.

"It was remarkably easy." Eliana laughed lightly, remembering. "I snuck into a bathroom on the main floor that no one ever uses, dyed and cut my hair, cleaned up the mess, donned my new uniform, and ducked in with a tour group passing through the palace. Then, *voilà!* Lina Smith was out on the streets of London, with hardly a penny to her name."

Elizabeth shook her head, impressed by Eliana's reckless boldness. "Weren't you scared?"

Eliana sat forward, her eyes shining. "I was exhilarated. For the first time in my life, I was free! I could go anywhere I wanted, do or say anything I wanted, live a normal life. I've learned so much, Elizabeth, I can't tell you. From people like you and Jess and Emily, from the people at the shelter, from everyone I've met. *Real* people."

"This explains a lot of things," Elizabeth exclaimed. "Your glasses, and your fancy nightgown. And that's why you've been brushing off David, because you're not really from Liverpool!"

"Right." Eliana smiled. "The poor dear fellow's homesick and wants nothing more than to chat about Liverpool. I've been so afraid he'd see through my masquerade. As for the opening night of Portia's play, remember when I was in such a rush to leave Mondo the other night?"

The puzzle pieces clicked. "We'd just spotted Princess Gloria, your big sister!"

Eliana nodded. "I can't risk bumping into her, or anyone else who might recognize me, and there are bound to be dozens of celebrities attending such an eagerly awaited premiere."

"But your sister, your family, the whole country . . . people are terribly worried about you," Elizabeth told Eliana. "You must be aware that there's a huge search on. They think you may have been kidnapped or killed! Maybe it's time for you to go back."

Eliana shook her head stubbornly. "It's too soon. There's still so much I want to discover! I couldn't do it, living in a palace with the paparazzi recording my every move. You just don't know how liberating it is to be Lina Smith! Besides," she added, "I've communicated with my family. They know I'm safe and not kidnapped. I don't understand why the newspapers are printing stories like that."

The two girls gazed at each other in silence. "So, what are you going to do about me, Elizabeth?" Eliana asked solemnly.

Elizabeth hesitated, her sense of duty dueling with sympathy and admiration for the young princess.

Seizing Elizabeth's hands, Eliana squeezed them tight. "Please," she begged. "Keep my secret. Let me be free for just a while longer."

For a long moment, Elizabeth looked deep into Eliana's sincere, pleading eyes. Then she nodded reluctantly. "I'll keep your secret, Eliana. I won't even tell my sister. But I'm warning you." Elizabeth couldn't help smiling. "David's not going to give up easily. He has a serious crush on you!"

Eliana threw her arms around Elizabeth. Elizabeth hugged her back. "Thank you, Elizabeth," the princess whispered, tears glimmering in her eyes. "Thank you, my true friend."

The last purple and orange glimmer of sunset was coloring the western sky as the twins, Gabriello, David, and Emily stepped out of their cab in front of the Ravensgate Theatre. A brightly lit marquee proclaimed opening night of *A Common Man*, starring British stage favorites Margaret Kent and Richard Winters.

A festive, elegantly dressed crowd filled the

lobby and spilled out onto the sidewalk. "The way Portia always talked, you'd have thought she was getting top billing," Emily said dryly as they made their way toward one of the ushers. "I bet she has a walk-on role with only one line."

"She probably plays a maid," Jessica said. "Or a cook. Wouldn't that be perfect?"

Handing them each a playbill, the usher showed them to their seats in the tenth row of the mezzanine. "They're great seats, anyway," remarked Elizabeth, sitting down in between Jessica and David. Tipping her head, she looked up at the glittering chandeliers and then over at the box seats festooned with rich velvet curtains. "I don't see how we can complain."

"Hullo, what's this?" Leafing through her playbill, Emily pointed to the cast of characters. "Portia's name isn't anywhere on here!"

Quickly, the others flipped to the same page. "'Peter Huntington is played by Richard Winters,'" read Jessica. "'Margaret Kent plays his wife, Genevra, and Penelope Abbott is their daughter, Isabel.' You're right, Em," she exclaimed. "Portia's not even down for any of the minor characters!"

Gabriello's dark eyebrows knotted in puzzlement. "Is this some kind of hoax?"

Just then the lights began to dim. Voices hushed and the last few people still standing in the aisles slipped hurriedly into their seats. "We'll just have to watch and see," Elizabeth whispered as the theater was plunged into darkness.

They held their breath as the red velvet curtain

slowly rose, revealing a tastefully decorated but not opulent drawing room. The figure of a man leaned against the mantel; a woman stood in the doorway, and a second woman reclined on a sofa.

Elizabeth's eyes took in the scene. She recognized the girl on the sofa just as Jessica's elbow jabbed into her side. "It's Portia!" Jessica hissed.

The play began with an argument between the "common man," Peter, his aristocratic and dissatisfied wife, and their spoiled, sharp-tongued daughter, Isabel . . . Portia.

Elizabeth watched, spellbound. Lounging, Isabel held a book at eye level, effectively blocking out her view of her father. She lowered the book only to address occasional disdainful remarks to her mother.

Every gesture and intonation was full of expression; the character was instantly full of life. "Portia's good—she's really good!" Elizabeth whispered to Jessica.

"She's fantastic," Jessica whispered back, "as much as I hate to admit it. But I still don't get it. Why does the program say Isabel is played by Penelope Abbott?"

"Maybe Portia is Penelope's understudy," Emily whispered from the other side of Jessica.

"Maybe," Elizabeth murmured, but she was dubious. That didn't make sense, either—the understudies' names were all listed, and Portia's wasn't among them.

Still puzzled, they sat back in their chairs to watch the gripping, fast-paced drama. As the minutes sped by, something peculiar happened. Elizabeth found herself anticipating some of Isabel's dry, sardonic lines; she could predict how the character would react in a given scene. *It's almost as if I've seen the play before,* she thought, bemused. *As if I knew Isabel . . .*

The play built up to a pre-intermission climax. Onstage, Isabel turned on her browbeaten father and blasted one of his humble suggestions with the scathing remark, "How quaint, Papa. Let's do."

How quaint . . . The little words echoed in Elizabeth's brain. Suddenly, she saw something, as clear as day.

"I figured it out!" she announced excitedly as soon as the curtain fell and the lights went up for intermission.

The applause died down and the audience poured out into the aisles, streaming toward the lobby. Elizabeth, Jessica, Emily, Gabriello, and David went out to the sidewalk for some fresh air.

"You figured out why Portia's name isn't in the playbill?" said David.

"No, something even more important," Elizabeth declared. "I've figured out Portia."

"How do you mean?" asked Emily.

"Didn't you notice?" Elizabeth prompted. "The first scene, when she was holding the book up so she wouldn't have to look at her father, and the scene where she was preparing for bed in an elaborate dressing gown, putting on eyeshades and earplugs to shut herself off from the world. Remember our first night at HIS, Jess?"

163

"Yeah, but—"

"And some of Isabel's lines," Elizabeth continued. "They were snotty things we've all heard *Portia* say around the dorm—nearly verbatim!"

David's eyes glinted with comprehension. "You're absolutely right. Portia is Isabel. Or should I say, Isabel is Portia?"

Elizabeth nodded eagerly. "She's been playing this part all along. Things she's said and done around the dorm—it's all been rehearsing. This isn't Portia's personality—it's Isabel's!"

Jessica and Emily both looked skeptical. "More likely, Portia just found the role she was born for," said Emily. "I never got the impression she didn't really mean it when she was being nasty to me!"

"We won't know until we go backstage after the play," Elizabeth conceded. *And perhaps meet the real Portia Albert for the first time!* she added to herself.

When the final curtain dropped, the standing-room-only crowd at Ravensgate Theatre leapt to their feet in an enthusiastic ovation. When Portia took her bow, dozens of bouquets rained down on the stage. Gathering an armful of flowers, she curtsied again and then darted behind the curtain.

Backstage pass in hand, the HIS crew hurried to congratulate their dormmate. They spotted Portia through an open dressing-room door, busy unpinning her hair.

Everyone but Elizabeth hung back. "I still don't trust her," Elizabeth heard Jessica murmur.

She waiked forward alone, her hand extended. "Portia, you were—"

Before Elizabeth could finish her sentence, Portia unexpectedly flung both arms around her. "I did it!" she cried. "Oh, thank you so much for coming!"

Realizing they weren't going to get their heads bitten off, Jessica, Emily, David, and Gabriello pressed forward to offer their congratulations. "You were great, Portia," Jessica gushed.

"You stole the show," David confirmed.

"I predict rave reviews," said Gabriello, "and a long, successful run."

"Oh, thank you, you all," Portia said tearfully. She patted Emily's arm. "I really wasn't sure until I went onstage tonight. I wasn't sure I could pull it off."

"But you were born to it, said Elizabeth. "You're a natural."

Portia's smile was wistful. "Do you think so? Does it appear that way to you?"

"Of course," said Jessica. "You're Sir Montford Albert's daughter, after all!"

Portia sighed. "Yes. Yes, I am."

"So, what's the story?" Emily demanded. "Why isn't your name in the playbill?" She pointed at the door to the dressing room. "And who's Penelope Abbott?"

"Penelope Abbott is . . . me." Portia waved toward a stack of folding chairs. "Maybe we should all sit down!"

As Elizabeth, Jessica, David, Gabriello, and Emily listened eagerly, Portia launched into a surprising tale. "I know you assumed that my father was the reason I landed a role in a big new West End play," she began. "You probably assumed that he pushed me into acting, and cheered me on every step of the way. Well, it wasn't exactly like that."

She dropped her eyes, and suddenly Elizabeth recalled their conversation of a few nights ago. "In fact, it was the opposite," Portia continued quietly. "The first time I told him I wanted to be an actress, he yelled at me. When I acted in little plays at school, he'd refuse to come and watch. When he finally did see me perform, instead of praising me or just saying something vaguely encouraging, he ridiculed me in front of everyone, telling me I had no talent."

"That's horrible!" Emily declared, her eyes flashing.

"You poor thing," murmured Elizabeth, her heart aching with sympathy.

"I believed him," Portia went on. "He was my father, after all, and the greatest living actor in England. Who would know talent if he didn't? But no matter how many times he cut me down, I couldn't shake my desire to be an actress. It's in the blood."

"So you left Edinburgh and came to London," said Elizabeth.

Portia nodded. "I came to London to throw myself body and soul into acting—to prove myself to him, to prove him wrong. I had to get away from him in order to do that. I had to get out from under his shadow . . . and his name. That's why I auditioned for parts as Penelope Abbott. I didn't want anyone, including my father, to claim I'd gotten a role because of his fame and influence."

"Well, you proved yourself tonight," Emily told her. "You're going to be a big star. And that's not idle flattery," she added dryly. "Frankly, none of us would go out of our way to butter you up!"

"I've been a witch, haven't I? There was so much at stake . . . my performance had to be perfect, down to the last gesture. But maybe I took my immersion in the role of Isabel too far. I never meant to alienate you. I hope it's not too late . . ."

Portia gave them a winsome, hopeful smile. It was impossible not to smile back. "To be friends?" finished Elizabeth. "Of course it isn't."

"Friends." Beaming, Portia leaned forward to give Jessica's hand a firm shake. "I promise I won't put on any more airs back at the dorm."

"Which reminds me." Jessica hopped to her feet and they all followed suit. "We'd better get moving if we don't want Mrs. Bates to lock us out. *Her* wicked witch imitation isn't an act!"

Chapter 12

As they'd arranged when they parted the afternoon before, Luke met Elizabeth and Jessica in front of HIS at eight o'clock sharp Friday morning.

Hoisting her duffel bag, Jessica turned to wave good-bye to her friends. "See ya, Em. Bye, Portia and Lina. Be good, David and Gabe!"

Mrs. Bates bustled out the front door to give each girl a brisk hug. "You'll be in good hands with the Pembrokes, my dears, but telephone if you won't be home by curfew Sunday eve. I'll worry myself sick, otherwise."

"Will do," Elizabeth promised. "Bye, everybody!"

Portia blew a kiss. Lina smiled at Elizabeth, holding one finger to her lips in a silent "don't tell" signal. Beyond them, in the front hall, Elizabeth caught a glimpse of a tall, dark-haired boy. Stepping to the door, Rene looked out at Elizabeth. At the sight of her overnight bag, and

Luke, he frowned, then turned away again without so much as a wave.

Elizabeth sighed. Rene had been giving her the cold shoulder for days, but what could she do? She'd tried her best to smooth things over with him, but if he didn't want to be friends . . .

They took a cab to Victoria Station and hurried directly to the ticket counter. "Robert's meeting us in Pembroke Woods," Jessica told Elizabeth and Luke. "He expects us to catch the nine-fifteen train—it takes about two hours, making a few stops on the way."

The agent, a wizened old man, peered at them through the ticket window. "Destination?"

"Pembroke Woods," said Elizabeth, pulling out her wallet. "Three seats, please."

"One way or return?"

For an instant, she hesitated. A strange premonition flooded over her, chilling the blood in her veins. *What if something happens to us? What if we go to Pembroke Manor . . . and don't come back?*

Don't be ridiculous, Elizabeth chastised herself. "Return, please," she replied briskly.

Tickets in hand, the three rushed to track nine, where the northwestbound train was already boarding. Climbing into a non-smoking car, they stowed their luggage overhead and sat down, Elizabeth and Jessica sitting next to each other on one side, with Luke in the seat by the window facing Elizabeth's.

A few minutes later, the train shuddered and

began rolling forward. Soon they were roaring out of London into lush green English farmland. "A weekend in the boring, safe countryside—this is going to be great," remarked Jessica, slumping so she could put her feet up on the empty seat next to Luke. "Aren't you guys relieved to get out of the city, to leave all that scary serial killer stuff behind?"

Elizabeth stared out the window. Again, for no earthly reason, she felt goose bumps prickling the skin on her arms. *Were* they leaving the danger, the evil, behind in London? She pictured the face of the gypsy fortune-teller as the old woman examined Jessica's palm. The gypsy saw something there—something that made her blanch and stutter. *Beware the full moon. . . .*

The full moon will follow us, Elizabeth realized, her eyes on the cloud-streaked sky. *Tonight it will shine as brightly over the village of Pembroke Woods as over London. . . .*

While Jessica regaled Luke with stories about the Pembroke family—stories she'd already forced her sister to listen to at least twice—Elizabeth continued to gaze pensively out the train window. *What a week it's been, and our internships at the* Journal *have only just begun!* she thought. The action had been nonstop: Dr. Neville's murder, Poo-Poo's mangled corpse, Lucy quitting over the alleged cover-up, Tony and Lucy's fight, Reeves naming Tony temporary crime editor. *And Luke . . . my friendship with Luke—our talks, our walks . . .*

Even dorm life had been far from dull. She'd bumped into an old flame, Rene Glize, only to

171

have a trivial misunderstanding spoil their chance at renewed friendship. Plain, ordinary Lina Smith had turned out to be the missing Princess Eliana. *Both Lina* and *Portia aren't who they seemed to be at first,* Elizabeth mused. *Everybody has their secrets, I guess.*

She glanced at Luke, who was smiling politely at Jessica's story. There was a visible tension about his body, in the tautness of his shoulders and the wariness in his eyes. *He knows it's not as simple as Jessica thinks, this escaping into the country,* Elizabeth guessed. They were almost certain there was a Pembroke connection to the murder of Dr. Neville . . . and at that very moment, they were on their way to Pembroke Manor.

Everybody has their secrets. And some secrets are darker than others. . . .

"There he is!" Jessica squealed as the train screeched to a stop in the quaint, tiny village of Pembroke Woods. "See? The tall dark-haired guy in the white shirt and ascot standing by the cool car. Isn't he gorgeous?"

The "cool car" was a silver Jaguar convertible. Elizabeth and Luke gaped.

Jessica was already on her feet, struggling to get her duffel bag out of the luggage compartment. The instant the door opened, she leaped out onto the platform. "Robert, hi!" she called, waving energetically.

Elizabeth and Luke followed at a slower pace. "I feel out of my element," Luke muttered nervously, putting a hand to his throat to loosen his necktie. "How am I going to know what to say to these people?"

"Don't worry," said Elizabeth. "You're ten times smarter than Robert Pembroke—according to Jessica, he was kicked out of just about every boarding school in Great Britain. Just be yourself and you'll charm the pants off all of them."

Luke gave her hand a quick, grateful squeeze. "Thanks, Elizabeth."

Robert strode forward to meet Jessica, relieving her of her duffel bag at the same time that he bent to brush her cheek with a kiss. "It's so wonderful to see you here," he proclaimed, his blue eyes glinting. "I can't wait to show you around our little corner of heaven."

Jessica smiled up at him, fluttering her eyelashes and looking as if she might swoon. Elizabeth and Luke exchanged a glance, rolling their eyes.

Collecting her wits, Jessica turned to present her sister to Robert. "In case you couldn't guess, this is my twin sister, Elizabeth. Oh, and her friend, Luke Shepherd—he works at the *Journal*."

Robert took Elizabeth's hand, flashing her an ultra-white, ultra-charismatic smile. "What a pleasure this is, Elizabeth. Jessica told me you were twins, but I really didn't believe it until now—I simply couldn't conceive of there being another girl as pretty as she is."

Elizabeth smiled back stiffly, taking an instant dislike to Robert Pembroke and his overdone, insincere flattery.

Facing Luke, Robert shook his hand next.

"Glad you could join us, old chap," he said in jovial, lord-of-the-manor style. "We'll have to chat about the newspaper business. You can bring me up to speed on goings-on at the *Journal*—it's a little Pembroke family operation, you know, and I really should be more in tune."

Luke nodded, his eyes intent on the other young man's face, as if he might be able to penetrate Robert's innermost thoughts. In the brief moment that they stood that way, Elizabeth was struck by the contrast they made. Though both were tall and well-built, with dark hair, fair complexions, and classic English features, any resemblance was only skin deep. Where Luke's manner was pure, open, and unpretentious, Robert's was artificial, arrogant, and condescending. *What does Jessica see in him?* Elizabeth wondered.

Oh, yeah—that, she thought as Robert led them over to the Jaguar. *The title, the money, the car, the estate. How could I forget?*

Robert unlocked the trunk of the car and tossed in Jessica's bag. "Put your things in the boot and hop in."

Luke held the back door for Elizabeth while Robert held the front passenger side door for Jessica. As she belted herself in, Jessica turned to flash a deliriously happy smile at her sister. *Isn't this the life?* her expression seemed to say.

Elizabeth smiled back with as much warmth as she could muster. No matter what she personally might think of Robert Pembroke, the fact was that her sister was crazy about him. *It's not fair to spoil*

Jessica's fun, she reminded herself. Besides, why not keep a positive attitude? No matter how snobby the Pembrokes might be, it was exciting to be in a beautiful new place . . . and with Luke at her side.

The Jaguar's powerful engine purred to life and Robert steered into the left lane of the narrow cobbled street that ran through the center of the village. With one hand, he gestured to the gray fieldstone cottages that lined the street, dark green ivy curling up around the doorframes. "These weavers' cottages were built in the sixteenth century," he informed his passengers. "This has always been sheep country."

They rumbled over a little wooden bridge. In the clear, bubbling brook below, a pair of large white swans glided majestically. "This pair and their ancestors have been coming here to raise their cygnets for a century or more," Robert said. "Hence the name of the local tavern."

Elizabeth laughed when she saw the weathered wooden sign swinging in the breeze over the door of the inn. "The White Swan—how appropriate!"

Rounding a bend, they left the village behind. On one side of the road, white sheep dotted lush green fields; on the other, woods swept upward toward high, forbidding moors. Through the trees, on the bank of another creek, Elizabeth spotted a ruined stone tower. "Look! What's that?" she called up to Robert.

"Woodleigh Abbey," he called back. "Or what's left of it. It's been a ruin for centuries—since it was burned during the Reformation, to be exact. They say it's haunted by the ghosts of four monks who perished in the conflagration."

Looking back over her shoulder, Elizabeth thought she glimpsed a ghostly form flitting through the trees. *It's just your overactive imagination, silly,* she chided herself, suppressing a shiver.

"It's all so beautiful," Jessica exclaimed.

Robert waved a hand in a proud, proprietary gesture. "It's all ours," he said simply. "We Pembrokes live a charmed life—always have. The land has been in the family for countless generations, passed down in unbroken succession to the oldest son." He grinned at Jessica. "Lucky me."

Lucky you is right. Elizabeth darted a sympathetic glance at Luke, who sat stiff and tense, his hands folded on his knees and his eyes fixed on the back of Robert's head. *How come some people have so much, and others so little?* she wondered. *What did Robert Pembroke do to deserve all this?*

The Jaguar crested a hill and Jessica caught her breath. "Is *that* Pembroke Manor?" she gasped in wonder.

Robert smiled, clearly pleased by her delight and awe. "Home sweet home."

The manor was constructed from the same gray fieldstone as the houses in the village, but on a far more splendid scale. It was shaped like a "U," with two wings extending forward on either side of a courtyard the size of a football field. *I bet it has a hundred rooms!* Jessica thought. *Eat your heart out, Lila—this makes Fowler Crest look like a gate-keeper's cottage!*

"I've never seen anything so magnificent," Jessica gushed. "It looks like someplace a king or queen might live."

"They've stayed as guests, anyway," Robert said nonchalantly. "Queen Victoria and her consort came here to hunt, and, back in the fifteenth century, one of the King Henrys stopped through. We had Malcolm, Gloria, and the rest of the current royal brood five or six summers ago. Boy, were we a wild bunch!"

They coasted to a stop in the circular drive. Out of nowhere, a uniformed groundskeeper appeared. Robert popped the trunk and stepped out of the car, leaving the keys in the ignition. Another servant was already pulling the luggage from the trunk.

Taking Jessica's hand, Robert gestured to Elizabeth and Luke. "Follow me." He pushed open a dark oak door two times as tall as Jessica and they stepped into a hallway as lofty and solemn as a cathedral. Both the floor and walls were gray stone; the ceiling was of blackened beams.

Jessica pointed to a large, ancient tapestry draping one wall. It depicted a shield divided into four quadrants, each containing a different emblem. "What's that?" she asked Robert.

"The Pembroke family crest. See the 'P' and 'R' intertwined? That's for Pembroke and 'Rex,' King, indicating the fealty of the Pembrokes to the royal family. The sword represents our willingness to do battle for crown and country. The water is

Woodleigh Falls—a symbol of the streams that flow through our land, making it rich and fertile. And the wolf is, for some reason I've never been able to figure out, our patron saint." He grinned. "Kind of a funny choice, considering we've always raised sheep. Perhaps early Pembrokes chose the wolf to honor and placate him, to bribe him to leave their flocks alone."

Jessica gazed in fascination at the coat of arms. Elizabeth also stared at the wolf, her eyes wide.

"I'll give you the grand tour presently," Robert promised as they proceeded down the hall. He stopped at a wide doorway. "First let's make the introductions. Hullo, anyone home?"

The room beyond was wide and bright, with tall casement windows standing open to the summer breeze. A table was set for lunch, and a buffet table next to the wall held an array of covered silver dishes. Four people dressed in elegant summer weekend clothes lounged by the windows, cocktail glasses in their hands.

"Mother, I'd like to reintroduce you to Jessica Wakefield." Robert slipped an arm around Jessica's waist, gently propelling her forward. "The crack reporter for the *Journal*, remember? And Jessica's sister, Elizabeth, and their friend, Luke."

With the smallest and coolest of smiles, Lady Pembroke extended one paper-thin hand. Jessica shook it gingerly, not wanting to crush the birdlike bones. "It's nice to see you again, Lady Pembroke. I'm glad you got your mink back."

"And my father."

Lord Pembroke bowed over Jessica's hand, squeezing it warmly. Jessica smiled, feeling an immediate liking for this gallant, distinguished older version of Robert. "Thank you for inviting us, Lord Pembroke."

"It's our pleasure, my dear," he assured her. Taking Elizabeth's hand, he repeated the sentiment. Then he shook Luke's hand. "What did you say your name was, young man?"

"Luke." Luke gazed deeply into the older man's eyes. "Luke Shepherd."

Lord Pembroke gave a start; his fingers tightened around Luke's, and something flickered behind his eyes. *Surprise?* Jessica wondered. *Recognition?* "Luke Shepherd," he muttered.

"Do you know the name, sir?" Luke asked pleasantly. "Perhaps because I work at the *Journal.*"

"Yes, that's it." Lord Pembroke's smile didn't quite reach his eyes. "Of course."

Liz should have brought Rene, Jessica thought, biting her lip. *Doesn't she see how common Luke is? Doesn't she realize he makes us look bad?*

Robert had turned to the other people in the room, a middle-aged man whom Jessica thought looked vaguely familiar and an attractive, young blond woman. "Joy and Andrew, how jolly to see you. I didn't realize you were joining us this weekend." With a flourish, Robert presented the pair to Jessica, Elizabeth, and Luke. "Our good family friend, Andrew Thatcher, and his fiancée, Joy Singleton."

That's how I know him—from that day at Dr.

Neville's, and the picture in the newspaper! Jessica thought, just as Elizabeth burst out, "Andrew Thatcher, the London chief of police?"

Andrew Thatcher smiled. "At your service."

Elizabeth and Luke exchanged a meaningful glance. Meanwhile, Joy Singleton shook Jessica's hand, giving her a friendly smile. "Robert Senior has promised us a ride this afternoon, and I'll make sure they put you on Cinnamon. She's my favorite mount—as gentle as a kitten and as comfortable as an easy chair."

Jessica smiled back, discreetly ogling Joy's butter-soft suede trousers, expensive casual silk shirt, and plentiful gold jewelry. "I'm not much of a rider—Cinnamon sounds perfect." *It all sounds perfect*, she thought blissfully. *It all looks perfect. It all* is *perfect.*

Robert rubbed his hands together. "I'm ravenous. What's for lunch?"

"Jessica appears to be having the time of her life," Luke observed to Elizabeth as they cantered along the bridle path a few horse-lengths behind the others.

"She is," Elizabeth agreed. Her sister was riding side-by-side with Robert. As Elizabeth watched, Robert leaned over to say something and Jessica tossed back her loose blond hair, laughing.

He's certainly treating her like a queen, Elizabeth conceded silently. *I can't fault him on that point.* Lord Pembroke Senior was also lavishing paternal attention on her, and Jessica had hit it off famously with the bubble-headed but pleasant Joy Singleton. "I don't think I've ever seen her fall so hard for a guy," Elizabeth remarked. "Although in this case, of course, it's not just the *guy*—she's infatuated with everything to do with the Pembrokes."

Abruptly, Luke reined in his horse, Nightwing. Sitting back in the saddle, Elizabeth slowed Lollipop, her mount, to a walk as well. "What is it?" she asked Luke.

Luke gestured to a trail that branched off from the main path and led into a grove of birch trees. "Let's go this way," he suggested. "I wouldn't mind sneaking away from the others."

If Elizabeth's cheeks hadn't already been flushed from the wind and sun, they would have turned pink at the thought of being alone with Luke in this enchanted place. "Let's," she agreed.

Dismounting, they led their horses to the verge of the wood, pausing to let Nightwing and Lollipop nibble at a clump of lush, tall grass.

A gust of wind swept down from the hills, stirring Elizabeth's hair and causing the grain in the fields to ripple like an ocean. Luke glanced back to where Jessica, Robert, Lord Pembroke Senior, Joy, and Andrew were just disappearing over the crest of a hill. "What do you think about Thatcher being here?" he asked Elizabeth.

Elizabeth tugged gently on Lollipop's reins. "It proves there's a close connection between him and Pembroke. Thatcher might very well put a muzzle on a police investigation at Pembroke's request."

181

"Right. And when we first arrived earlier, didn't Lord Pembroke Senior strike you as a bit . . . edgy?"

"As if he were guilty of something," Elizabeth agreed, "like covering up a murder."

"At the very least," she thought she heard Luke mutter. More loudly, he said, "Yes, it certainly looks like it's going to be an interesting weekend."

Leading the horses, they strolled into the grove of birches. Waving gently in the breeze, the trees cast a dappled pattern of sun and shadow upon the path. Elizabeth breathed deeply of the damp, ferny scent. "I'm glad Jessica talked me . . . us . . . into coming with her," she said, glancing at Luke with a shy smile.

He smiled back. "So am I. Here, let's tether the horses and explore."

Looping the reins around the branches of a tree, Luke reached for Elizabeth's hand. "Do you hear a stream?" he asked.

Cutting off the path, they waded through the ferns in the direction of the sound of running water, still holding hands. Elizabeth's heart pounded with anticipation . . . of precisely what, she wasn't sure. *Something, though,* she knew, her blood feeling hot in her veins. *Something is going to happen between us. . . .*

They came to the banks of the stream, and suddenly Luke stopped. Dropping Elizabeth's hand, he bent to examine a bushy plant growing under the birches. "What is it?" Elizabeth asked.

Luke ran a finger along the petals of one of the

182

strange, hooded white flowers. "Wolfsbane," he said somberly. His gaze locked onto Elizabeth's and a hot spark shot between them. "According to medieval lore, it blooms when it's time for the werewolf to come out."

Elizabeth had been about to pick one of the unusual flowers. Now she drew back her hand as if she'd been stung, her eyes shadowed with dread.

"It's all right." Luke stepped close to her, one arm wrapping protectively around her shoulders. Sliding the other hand into his trouser pocket, he pulled out a tarnished silver pendant on a chain. "See this symbol?"

Tentatively, Elizabeth touched the pendant. "It's a wolf's head, with a five-sided star."

"The pentagram is an ancient, magical symbol of immense power, did you know that? Here, the werewolf is inside it. It will contain and neutralize his power." Lifting his hands, Luke clasped the chain around Elizabeth's neck. "Wear this at all times, and it will protect you."

The pendant was cold against her bare skin . . . and yet, somehow, warm at the same time. *I can feel it,* she thought, staring up at Luke with wide, mesmerized eyes. *I can feel the power.*

"It will protect you," Luke repeated softly. His hands lingered on her neck; he tilted her face toward his. "And *I* will protect you."

Slowly, he bent his head to hers. A sudden, fierce hunger swept through Elizabeth's body and she went to him eagerly. At last, their lips met in the kiss they'd both been dreaming of all week long.

Chapter 13

"I really wish we'd made friends with Portia in time to borrow some of her clothes for this trip," Jessica said mournfully, twisting to examine herself in the full-length mirror. "This dress is OK in Sweet Valley, but somehow it doesn't seem right for a formal dinner at Pembroke Manor."

Elizabeth flung up her hands. Jessica had brought four dresses with her, and tried on every one of them twice. "We'll miss dinner altogether if you don't hurry and make up your mind. You could always just put on your nightgown and go straight to bed!"

Jessica sighed. Lila and Amy had helped her pick out the cherry-red, square-necked dress—it *was* the most elegant, grown-up dress she'd ever owned, and fancier than Elizabeth's sailor dress. "I guess with a single strand of pearls, it will do," she decided. "But I'm sure Joy will look a thousand times nicer."

"Probably," Elizabeth said without much sympathy. "She's the type who has a closet full of designer originals and spends all her time thinking about what outfit to put on next."

"Really, Liz, you're such a reverse snob," Jessica accused, slipping her feet into a pair of black patent leather sling-backs. "Joy's a perfectly nice person—you'd find that out if you gave her half a chance." She paused at the dressing table to spritz herself behind the ears and on the wrists with perfume, then breezed toward the door. "I'm ready!"

Luke and Robert, both wearing jackets and ties, were already standing in the entrance to the large, imposing dining room. "Look at that *table*," Jessica hissed to Elizabeth. "It's fifty feet long!"

"You need a bullhorn to ask for the butter," Elizabeth hissed back.

Just then, Lord and Lady Pembroke approached from the drawing room, walking arm-in-arm. Andrew Thatcher and Joy Singleton followed. *Joy's in* sequins, Jessica thought with envy and dismay. *And, wow, can she carry it off.*

Robert took Jessica's hand, slipping it through the crook of his arm. "May I have the honor?"

Jessica nodded, smiling up at him. With the last rays of sunset shooting like golden arrows through the windows, Robert looked more like a fairy tale prince than ever. As they walked into the dining room, she couldn't even feel the floor under her feet. Only Robert's arm kept her connected to earth. *This is how it will be,* she thought, *walking together down the aisle of the village church on our wedding day. . . .*

186

Robert pulled out a chair for Jessica. On the other side of the table, Luke did the same for Elizabeth. The instant all eight were seated, two uniformed maidservants materialized out of nowhere, one filling crystal goblets with ice water and the other placing flat, broad-rimmed bowls of creamy lobster bisque in front of each diner.

Jessica started to reach for a spoon and then shot a glance, half amused and half panicked, at her sister. *Two knives, three spoons, and four forks . . . what are we going to be eating here?* Out of the corner of her eye, she saw Lady Pembroke select a spoon and mirrored the choice.

"We had the nicest horseback ride this afternoon, Lady Pembroke," Jessica said, smiling at her hostess. "I wish you could have joined us."

Lady Pembroke laughed dryly. "I don't ride, my dear. But I'm glad you enjoyed your little tour of the property."

"We only saw half of it," Robert told his mother. "We'll have to ride out in the other direction tomorrow."

"Can we ride to Woodleigh Abbey?" Joy asked. "I'd love to explore the ruins."

"Didn't Andrew tell you about the ghosts?" Robert teased. "Even in broad daylight, Woodleigh can be a disconcerting place."

"Oh, I don't worry about such things when Andrew's along," said Joy, dimpling. "Do you really think the ghost of a meek old monk would stand up to the London chief of police?"

Robert laughed heartily. Lord Pembroke

chuckled. "Such fearlessness," he said. "Perhaps you should join the force yourself, Joy, my dear."

"I've considered it," Joy replied in a bantering tone.

"Or she could report for the *Journal*," Robert suggested, one eyebrow cocked ironically. "Uncovering the wicked truths of the world takes fearlessness, too."

"That it does," his father agreed. There was an unexpected note of seriousness in his voice, but it vanished as he turned to speak to Jessica. "I haven't heard, my dear, how you and your sister are finding your summer internships at the newspaper."

"Oh, we love it," Jessica declared, looking to Elizabeth for confirmation. "It's so exciting! Our very first case, at Dr.—"

Elizabeth shot her a warning look, and Jessica bit off the sentence. *We weren't supposed to be there. We're not supposed to know anything,* she reminded herself. "At Lady Wimpole's," she amended, toying with her soup spoon. "And then, of course, the mink thing at Pembroke Green, when I met Robert. It was quite a day. What I started to say is that we're very sorry about the death of your friend, Dr. Neville."

"Oh, yes, well . . ." Lord Pembroke exchanged a glance with Andrew Thatcher. Then his eyes darted to his son. Robert sipped his soup, oblivious.

Maybe I'm not even supposed to know they're friends. Jessica bit her lip. She couldn't remember—her mind had gone blank. *What can I say and what can't I?*

Elizabeth came to the rescue. "Robert told us

Dr. Neville was your best friend," she said softly. "We're truly sorry."

"Thank you, my dear," Lord Pembroke said gruffly. "It's quite a loss, quite a loss."

At that moment one of the servants, who'd been performing her duties in absolute silence, stepped to Lord Pembroke's side and cleared her throat timidly. "Excuse me, sir, but there's a visitor. Constable Pickering. He says . . . it's urgent business."

Dropping his crumpled cloth napkin on the table, Lord Pembroke rose to his feet. "Urgent? I can't imagine—well, bring him in, bring him in. We'll find out what's on his mind and offer him dinner."

Lady Pembroke frowned. "Really, darling. The local *constable*, for dinner?"

Lord Pembroke waved at her. "Hush, Henrietta."

The constable entered the dining room, his hat in his hands. Jessica and the others gaped at him, curious. *Something's wrong,* Jessica guessed instantly. *That man's as white as one of Woodleigh Abbey's ghosts!*

"I'm sorry to interrupt. Perhaps, Lord Pembroke . . ." Constable Pickering shot an uncomfortable glance at Lady Pembroke. "Perhaps we could have a word . . . alone."

"It's all right, Pickering," Lord Pembroke assured him somewhat impatiently. "Just tell us your news so we can get on with our meal."

With visible reluctance, the constable complied. "It's the sheep, sir."

Lord Pembroke's dark eyebrows shot up. "The sheep?"

"The flock in the northeast pasture. A villager out potshotting rabbits along your property line found them, just at sunset. Four of them."

"Found them . . . ?"

"Dead," Constable Pickering said flatly. "Their throats torn right out. Hard to say if it was the work of man or beast."

Lord Pembroke sat back down as if the wind had been knocked out of him. Somebody dropped a soup spoon with a clatter. Jessica stared at the constable and then ran her wide, horrified eyes around the table. All present had turned pale with shock and revulsion.

Jessica gripped the arms of her chair. The room was spinning around her; she knew she was on the verge of fainting. *Dead with their throats torn out,* she thought. *Just like Poo-Poo and the nurse and Dr. Neville . . .*

Understandably, the dinner party broke up early. No one much felt like playing cards or charades. "I'm sorry your first night at Pembroke Manor hasn't been more fun," Robert said to Jessica as they strolled through the manicured English gardens.

Jessica glanced up at the black sky. Shreds of tattered clouds raced along, momentarily obscuring the round, full moon. "Are—are you sure we're . . . safe out here?" she asked Robert, shivering in the jacket he'd lent her.

The manicured English gardens were set in the courtyard, surrounded on three sides by the house. "Safe as if you were tucked in your own bed," Robert promised. "The outside gate is locked. Besides . . ." He reached out, pulling her toward him. "I'm here with you, aren't I?"

Jessica wrapped her arms around Robert's waist and lifted her face to his. Robert bent his head and their mouths met in a deep, searching kiss. "Yes," Jessica whispered. "Oh, yes."

Robert hugged her tightly, his lips moving to her throat. "So, don't worry about the sheep." He nibbled lightly on her ear. "Most likely, it was just the work of local youths, out looking for trouble. The constable will get to the bottom of it in the morning."

Above, the wind pushed the clouds aside. Suddenly, the gardens were bathed in the pale, silver light of the full moon. *Maybe it was just local kids,* Jessica thought. *But maybe not. Maybe the danger isn't limited to London—maybe it followed us here.*

"Elizabeth and Luke think . . ."

"What?" Robert asked, kissing her cheek, her temple, her forehead.

She'd been about to tell him Elizabeth and Luke's werewolf theory. All at once, though, she realized how silly it would sound. *Elizabeth and Luke have gone completely off their rockers. There's no such thing as werewolves—any sane person knows that!* Anyway, who wanted to think about werewolves when Robert Pembroke, the richest, handsomest boy in all of England, was driving her crazy with kisses?

"Elizabeth and Luke think I'm incredibly lucky to have met you," Jessica murmured. "And on *that* topic, I agree with them one hundred percent."

Lord and Lady Pembroke and Andrew and Joy had retired upstairs, leaving Elizabeth and Luke alone in the parlor. They'd pulled the sofa close to the hearth, but despite a roaring fire, Elizabeth couldn't seem to get warm.

Outside, the wind howled relentlessly. Something tapped against the window, making them both jump.

"It's OK," Luke said soothingly. "It was just a tree branch."

He wrapped an arm around Elizabeth's shoulders and she pressed her head against him. "There's something out there," Elizabeth whispered. She could sense it lurking in the windy dark, encircling the manor like the evening mist. "Something terrible, something evil."

Luke touched her chin, then traced his finger down her throat to the pendant he'd given her that afternoon. "You're safe with this," he reminded her. "And with me. We're safe here, inside."

Suddenly, they heard a crashing sound. Elizabeth jumped from Luke's arms, her heart in her throat.

The wind had blown one of the casement windows open; it banged against the wall, the curtain fluttering. Leaping to her feet, Elizabeth raced to shut it. The cold air sliced through her clothes, carrying a scent of the wild moors. *The moors, where the werewolf roams, hunting for his next victim. . . .*

With both hands, she pushed against the window. Just then, she heard a wailing sound in the distance. Was it the call of a bird? A dog barking?

Luke stepped up behind her and wrapped his arms around her waist. Elizabeth leaned back against him, closing her eyes. "We're safe . . . inside," he repeated, his lips against her hair. "But don't venture out there, Elizabeth, even for a breath of fresh air. Keep your windows tightly shut."

"The slaughtered sheep," she whispered. "It was the werewolf, wasn't it?"

She felt him nod. "He's strong and hungry," said Luke. "Stay inside, Elizabeth. The moon is full—this is his night. The werewolf's night . . ."

Somewhere in the house, a clock struck midnight as Elizabeth padded down the hall in her nightgown and robe to Jessica's bedroom. *Why did the Pembrokes give us rooms so far apart?* she wondered, suddenly wishing she and Jessica were sharing a room.

Reaching the door, she tapped lightly. "Come in," Jessica called.

At the sound of her sister's voice, Elizabeth's knees buckled with relief. She pushed open the door.

Jessica was sitting at the dressing table, brushing out her hair. "What are you doing up, Liz?" she asked cheerfully.

"I knew you and Robert went for a walk in the gardens, and I just wanted to make sure you—you got back in safely," she stammered. "It's such a creepy night." *And I don't trust him,* she added silently to herself.

Like Elizabeth's, the room was darkly paneled, with heavy velvet curtains draping both the windows and the antique four-poster bed. Jessica had lit some candles, and in the flickering light, the portraits of long-gone Pembrokes hanging on the walls seemed almost to glow with life, to breathe.

Shivering, Elizabeth sat down on the edge of Jessica's bed, pulling the coverlet around her legs. "Did you have a nice walk?"

"Oh, it was wonderful," said Jessica, stars in her eyes. "Robert is . . . wonderful. Isn't he? And this house—isn't it awesome? Robert says it takes a full-time staff of *ten* people just to keep it running."

"Hmm," Elizabeth murmured.

"Wasn't the ride this afternoon fun? I just think the Pembrokes are so nice. And Joy is great, isn't she? So elegant and well-bred. Doesn't it seem silly to you now?"

"Doesn't what seem silly?" asked Elizabeth.

"Your conspiracy theory. Your werewolf theory." Jessica laughed. "Really, to think that all those random bad things are connected somehow, and that the Pembrokes have anything to do with it!"

"They *are* connected," Elizabeth insisted. "The facts haven't changed, Jessica."

Jessica waved her hairbrush dismissively. "You and your pale boyfriend are wrong about the Pembrokes, just plain wrong. Go to sleep, Liz. You were scaring each other with spook stories—I can tell. You'll come around and see things my way in the light of day."

There was no point arguing. "Good night, Jess," Elizabeth said, crossing to the door.

"Good night."

Back in her own room, Elizabeth sat down at the cherry writing desk. Opening a drawer, she found a neat stack of creamy stationery and some pens. "I don't feel the least bit tired," she reflected out loud. "I'll write a letter to Todd. I really have been neglecting my correspondence with him. . . ."

Taking a sheet of paper, she uncapped a pen and scrawled a line. "Dear Luke," she wrote.

Her mistake jumped out at her, stinging like a slap across the face. Elizabeth bit her lip, flooded with guilt. She could still feel Luke's passionate good-night kiss, searing her whole body like a flame.

Oh, Todd, I'm sorry. I just don't know what I'm doing. She crumpled the paper and tossed it into the wastebasket. Turning off the light switch, she ran across the cold wood floors and jumped into bed.

The sheets were like ice; Elizabeth tucked her feet up under her nightgown, shivering. Pulling the covers up to her chin, she stared out into the shadowy room with wide-awake eyes.

How will I ever be able to sleep? she wondered. Outside, the wind had picked up. The windows rattled; a draft made the curtains stir. And the full moon was shining right into the room. So bright, so revealing . . .

Elizabeth tossed in the big bed, her eyelids fluttering. She struggled to wake, to shake herself free of the nightmare, but in vain. She was captured by the dream, helpless.

In it, she ran through Pembroke Manor, searching for someone. First she flew into the dining room, only to find the table smashed, broken china and glass everywhere, and the white linen tablecloth spattered with blood.

Her heart pounding, she dashed into the parlor. The fire was dead; the windows flapped open in the wind.

Where is she? Elizabeth wondered, running, running.

Jessica's bedroom was empty, the velvet hangings ripped from the bed and the sheets tumbled. *The garden,* Elizabeth remembered. *They went for a walk in the garden. She's alone with him. . . .*

She burst out into the courtyard, and plunged into the maze constructed of tall, pruned hedges. She ran right and then left, left again, and then right . . . in circles . . . *I'll never reach her,* she thought, tears streaming from her eyes as she tried to claw her way through the hedge. *I'll never find my way out. . . .*

Suddenly, the hedges dissolved. Elizabeth found herself in a dim corridor, face-to-face with royal figures from the sixteenth century. They were silent and stiff and lifeless—*the wax museum!* she realized.

She knew she was almost there. Dashing forward, she rounded a corner. And there was her sister! "Jessica!" Elizabeth screamed.

But Jessica didn't hear; she turned and fled, her blond hair billowing. At that moment, a wax figure came to life and sprang after her. Elizabeth saw a glint of red eyes—a pointed snout and the flash of white fangs dripping with blood—an elongated, hairy, powerful body . . .

The werewolf. The werewolf was after Jessica!

Elizabeth ran, knowing she had to reach her sister before the werewolf did. She heard voices behind her—strangely enough, the voices of young Robert Pembroke and Rene Glize— but although they seemed to be calling to her, she didn't slow down. "Beware the full moon!" Rene shouted. "Beware the full moon!" Robert echoed.

Her eyelids felt as heavy as lead; Elizabeth lifted them with an effort.

The dim, gray light of a misty dawn filled the strange bedroom. Elizabeth blinked, disoriented. Then she remembered where she was: Pembroke Manor.

And she remembered her horrible dream—the reason her sleep had been fitful and unsatisfying.

Jessica, Elizabeth thought, pushing back her covers.

An immediate, instinctive fear for her sister's well-being seized Elizabeth's heart in a viselike grip. She knew Jessica wouldn't appreciate being awakened at the crack of dawn, especially after she'd stayed up so late, but Elizabeth just had to see her. She had to make sure she was all right.

In bare feet and with her nightgown flying, Elizabeth ran down the hall to Jessica's bedroom. The door was ajar; she burst through it.

As in her dream, one of the curtains that draped the four-poster bed had been ripped down. A body lay on top of the tumbled sheets, facedown, its blond hair swirling across the pillow.

The girl wasn't asleep. Her limbs were twisted at an unnatural angle, and she was too still . . . too still. And the blood . . .

The sheets were white no longer, but soaked with scarlet blood. Elizabeth couldn't see the face, the throat, but she knew . . . she knew. The scream exploded from the very center of her being, splitting her in two. "Jessica!"

She screamed again, and again, wordless shrieks of infinite agony. A few seconds later, Luke rushed into the room, still in pajamas, his dark hair tousled. Running straight to the bed, he took the pale wrist between his thumb and forefinger, feeling for a pulse. For a moment that seemed to last forever, he waited. Then he dropped the wrist, shaking his head.

Hastening back to Elizabeth's side, Luke

clasped her tightly in his arms. She buried her face against his chest, brokenhearted sobs wracking her body. Luke stroked her hair, whispering, "Ssh. Ssh."

But Elizabeth knew her tears would never end; her pain and sorrow could never be soothed. Her beloved twin sister was dead—*murdered*!

Don't miss Sweet Valley High #105, **A Date with a Werewolf**, *the second book in this thrilling three-part miniseries.*

Bantam Books in the Sweet Valley High series
Ask your bookseller for the books you have missed

SIGN UP FOR THE SWEET VALLEY HIGH® FAN CLUB!

Hey, girls! Get all the gossip on Sweet Valley High's® most popular teenagers when you join our fantastic Fan Club! As a member, you'll get all of this really cool stuff:

- Membership Card with your own personal Fan Club ID number
- A Sweet Valley High® Secret Treasure Box
- Sweet Valley High® Stationery
- Official Fan Club Pencil (for secret note writing!)
- Three Bookmarks
- A "Members Only" Door Hanger
- Two Skeins of J. & P. Coats® Embroidery Floss with flower barrette instruction leaflet
- Two editions of *The Oracle* newsletter
- Plus exclusive Sweet Valley High® product offers, special savings, contests, and much more!

Be the first to find out what Jessica & Elizabeth Wakefield are up to by joining the Sweet Valley High® Fan Club for the one-year membership fee of only $6.25 each for U.S. residents, $8.25 for Canadian residents (U.S. currency). Includes shipping & handling.

Send a check or money order (do not send cash) made payable to "Sweet Valley High® Fan Club" along with this form to:

SWEET VALLEY HIGH® FAN CLUB, BOX 3919-B, SCHAUMBURG, IL 60168-3919

NAME _____
(Please print clearly)

ADDRESS _____

CITY_____ STATE _____ ZIP_____
(Required)

AGE _____ BIRTHDAY_____ / _____ / _____

Life after high school gets even sweeter!

Jessica and Elizabeth are now freshman at Sweet Valley University, where the motto is: Welcome to college – welcome to freedom!

Don't miss any of the books in this fabulous new series.

♡ College Girls #1 ....56308-4 $3.50/4.50 Can.
♡ Love, Lies and Jessica Wakefield #2........56306-8 $3.50/4.50 Can.